RUNNING AWAY

catherine mede

FLYING KIWI
PRESS

Running Away
© 2016 by Catherine Mede
Publisher: Flying Kiwi Press
Cover Design: Copyright 2016 © Dwell Design and Press/ Kate
Strawbridge

Disclaimer: The characters and events in this book are the creation of the author, and resemblance to persons, whether living or dead, is strictly coincidental.

Businesses, towns and places are used as settings and have no relation to any event or actually happening outside the authors' imagination.

Amazon ISBN 978-0-473-37570-6
ePub ISBN 978-0-473-37569-0
pdf ISBN 978-0-473-37571-3
Paperback ISBN 978-0-473-37568-3

Dedication

To Deborah
A bestie in the truest sense of the word.
Thank you for being with me when I created this story.
Amazing how inspiring tramping can be.
There is such a thing as love a second time around.
Love you x x x

Chapter One

8:15pm - Tuesday, Nelson, New Zealand

Larissa Greene yawned violently as she opened the front door of her flat and put her keys on the tray in the hallstand. Her handbag fell from her slumped shoulder and she swung it onto the table.

Another long day at work, her eyes were sore from staring at the computer screen for so long. She rubbed them as she sniffed, hoping to smell something nice for dinner.

It was 8pm, and the last thing she wanted to do was cook.

She walked down the hallway and into the kitchen. Bowls and plates were strewn across the bench, a half washed frying pan lay on its side in the sink, the hot tap dribbling. She ground her teeth as she twisted the tap - it hadn't been turned off properly. That would mean a higher electricity bill and a higher water bill.

She took a deep breath to try and calm herself. *No point getting upset now.*

Nothing edible sat in the fridge - a block of stale cheese, milk, several bottles of Diet Coke, half a dozen cans of beer. The oven lay empty and cold.

Nothing had been cooked.

"Die you bastard. Die." She heard a voice mutter from the lounge.

1

She clenched her fists tightly as she stormed into the lounge where Gerald lay sprawled across the couch, controller in hand. His body was covered with remnants of corn chips and crumbs littered the floor around him. On his slightly greying head, he wore headphones with a microphone attached. No doubt talking to the other gamer.

"Gerald!" she yelled. He continued to hammer away at the controller, pushing the buttons furiously as he sat up and leaned towards the large flat screen television that dominated the small lounge. She leaned over the velour couch and tapped his shoulder, trying to get his attention.

"For god's sake Rissy, shush!" He waved a hand in her direction as he continued to beat up his onscreen opponent.

Larissa ground her teeth. She'd never liked that nickname that he had given her, and right now, she hated it even more. She moved from behind the couch, between the coffee table and in front of the television screen.

"Rissy! Move outta my way!"

"No." She planted her hands on her hips as she glared at him. He used his hands to push the air in front of him, hoping that she would move as well. Instead, she reached behind her and flicked off the screen.

"Whaddya do that for? Come on Rissy, I was winning."

"I don't care if the Pope was winning!"

"Come on Rissy, don't be like that."

"Like what? Tell me, what am I being like?"

"Rissy, what's up? Rough day at work?"

Larissa twitched her lips. "Nope, not really?" She said through clenched teeth.

"Then tell me, what's wrong?"

"What have you done today?" She asked, glaring at him.

"Whaddya mean? I put out the trash, I cleaned the kitchen..."

"Cleaned the kitchen? That kitchen doesn't look like anyone has been near it in a week."

"I did clean it. Then I had lunch."

Larissa snorted. "You're an unemployed bum. You haven't vacuumed the floor, look at it. This room stinks. The curtains need to be opened, and what did you make for tea? You've been on the XBox all day haven't you?"

"Time ran away on me sweetheart. I had planned on doing those things. There's nothing wrong with being on the XBox," Gerald whined.

"Nothing wrong! You lazy, good for nothing piece of shit. Get out."

"Come on Rissy, babe, you can't do that to me."

Larissa swiped her hand over the television and the screen, holding up the dust encrusted fingers.

"You're too busy playing all the time. You don't pull your weight around here, I earn all the money and you do nothing to help out. You've been unemployed for nearly a year! When was the last time you *looked* for a job? If you didn't work, you could at least look after this place while I bust my ass all day and half of the night just for you to buy more bloody games! And when was the last time you did anything decent for me?"

"I brought you flowers the other day. Picked them 'specially for you."

"You picked them from the neighbour's garden!"

"It's the thought that counts."

"No it isn't. You're cheap and lazy, and to be honest, I've had enough. Now pack your things and go."

He remained where he was, so Larissa went into the kitchen, grabbed a fistful of plastic bags and took them into their bedroom and proceeded to throw his clothes into the bags. He didn't have a lot, so there wasn't much to pack. Four bags later, she went into the lounge to find Gerald had turned the television on and was playing his game again.

Five nights of working late, all she wanted when she got home was peace and quiet, a place to put her feet up and a nice cooked meal, without her having to do any of the work. Instead, for the last six months, she had come home, often late, proceeded to clean the house, cook tea, and made sure that Gerald was happy.

Not anymore. She'd had enough. Larissa walked over to the window, made sure he was watching her as she opened it, and threw the four bags out.

"Come on, whaddya do that for?"

"Duh!" Larissa shook her head, and went back to the television, turning it off again. She unplugged the XBox and picked it up off the TV stand. As she moved to throw it out the window, Gerald grabbed it from her hands, holding it protectively in his arms.

Gerald put the controller down and looked at her, studying her. She could see the thoughts running through his head. Menstruation cycle - he raised his eyes. It was enough to tip her over the edge.

"No, I haven't got my period, you Neanderthal." She turned, picked up the large screen television and stumbled over to the window. She heard Gerald rush up behind her. She got to the window, and tilted the television; it slowly eased outside before falling, just out of Gerald's reach.

She dusted her hands and watched as Gerald leaned out the window to view the damage.

"You crazy bitch!"

"Yip, crazy as. Now move your arse out that door!"

He hesitated, a moment too long. He narrowed his eyes at her.

"Hang on a minute, Rissy, sweetheart," he paused, looking at Larissa as his shoulders heaved. He was going to try and sweet talk her. She crossed her arms, waiting.

"Honey, how about we get pizza for tea, my shout. Come on, sit down, and relax."

"Why should I sit down? The house needs to be cleaned. Are you going to clean it?"

"No, why would I do that?" Too late, he realised his mistake and Larissa felt somewhat vindicated when he went from sweetness to defensive.

"What has gotten into you, Rissy? You've been working late for the last five nights, are you tired? You normally come home and cook tea, but tonight..."

Larissa screeched loudly. It was the final straw. Something snapped inside of her. She had put up with his bullshit for so long, being fobbed off, having him defensively defending his lack of jobs, his not doing housework, or cooking, or even trying to do any of those things. She rushed into the kitchen and grabbed a bread knife from the drawer. Brandishing it and yelling like a banshee, she ran into the lounge. Gerald saw the flash of steel and ran around the couch, trying to avoid her.

"My name is Larissa, not Rissy. I'm over playing games. I'm over catering to you. The door's that way!" She pointed to the front door glaring at Gerald as she huffed and puffed, her hair falling wildly around her face.

"You're insane!" he yelled as he slammed the door.

"Yes I bloody am! Insane to have ever let you into my life!" Her shoulders rose and fell as she breathed, and she let the knife slip from her hands. Had she really chased Gerald out of the house with a knife?

She giggled, nervously. As her breathing calmed, exhaustion took its place. She fell onto the crumb coated couch, staring at where the television had been.

She shouldn't have thrown it out.

She'd bought it.

Tears sprang to her eyes.

Chapter Two

8am - Wednesday, Nelson, New Zealand

Red-eyed and shoulders drooping, she arrived at work. Placing her handbag on the floor under her desk and tucking it under with her feet she turned on her computer, ready to start her day. She rubbed her eyes with the back of her hand, trying to be gentle and not smudge her makeup, which she couldn't get applied very well today. Instead of her usual sleek look, her makeup made her look like a worn out hooker.

She hadn't slept well overnight, expecting Gerald to come flying in through the door, but he hadn't. She didn't regret kicking him out as she had long since gotten over the affection she had felt for him... but her bed was cold and empty without another body to share it with. She had cried herself to sleep, cuddling her childhood teddy bear that always got pulled out of the wardrobe for any such an emergency.

Poor teddy had been out a lot since she turned 22. Relationships, meaningful ones, had eluded her, and she was moving into her thirties worried that she would end up being lonely, old and alone.

"Morning Larissa." Trudy interrupted her thoughts as she pranced through to her office.

"Hmmm," Larissa replied, but Trudy didn't take any notice. Sitting at her computer, Larissa looked through the door into Trudy's office, at the file sitting on her desk. She had stayed at work until eight pm to get it finished, hence the fight with

Gerald. Trudy picked up the file, flicked through the pages, nodding her head. She didn't look up or acknowledge that Larissa had done the work she had requested. Instead, she put it down, picked up the phone and started dialling. Larissa pulled up the typing that she had for the day and started getting it done.

"Good morning Linda," Paul said as he passed by her desk. She sighed as she returned his greeting. In the five years she had worked at the office, Paul hadn't once got her name right. He had called her everything from Lacey to Lynette. The closest he got to her name was Lysandra.

Instead of closing the door, like he normally did, he left it open and sat in the chair opposite Trudy. Larissa couldn't help but overhear the conversation that went on.

"Did you do that report last night, for me?" Paul asked.

"Yes, finished it late last night," Trudy replied. Larissa could imagine her batting her heavily mascara-ed eyelashes at him. She did see the file being picked up and passed over the desk. The same file that she had worked on.

There was a moment of silence, where Paul must have flicked through the file before he spoke. "Excellent, looks like you have really worked hard on this."

"Thank you, Paul. As I said, I worked until quite late just to make sure that it was done by this morning for your meeting."

"I appreciate the effort, Trudy, you're so efficient, I love that about you."

"Oh, thank you, Paul, gotta make you look great, don't we."

"You do that, my dear." A shuffling of material told Larissa that Paul was rising from his seat. He breezed out of the office with a big grin on his face, moving so quickly that Larissa didn't get a chance to correct his assumption that Trudy had done the report.

Trudy danced as she came out of her office. "Oh my goodness, Paul was so pleased with that report." She looked out the window at the cars in the park below. There was a moment of heavy silence, as Larissa waited for Trudy to thank her for her work, but it didn't come.

She turned back to her typing, pounding at the keys like they were Trudy's head. She hated that her boss took all her credit, and didn't bother to rectify everyone's assumption that it was actually Larissa's work.

~∞~

12:45pm - Wednesday

By lunch time, Larissa had managed to calm herself down enough to ring Julie, her bestie.

"You did what?" Julie's laughter was contagious. She needed this.

"I know, I threatened him with a bread knife. You should have seen that sucker run! His tail was well and truly tucked between his legs," Larissa said.

"Man, wish I had seen that, and you chucking that TV out the window! Why'd you do that?"

"Goodness, I don't know, I was just over it. Sick of him turning it on to play games, so I just threw it out the window."

Julie laughed so hard she snorted, and both of the girls started snorting at each other down the phone.

"I needed that, thanks Jules."

"Hey Lari, anything for you my friend. How's work going today?"

"Don't get me started on that! I want to go back to work in a semi-good mood."

"That bad, huh. Why don't you find yourself a decent job? You're the most underpaid over-utilised legal executive I know."

Larissa sighed. She knew that she should really look for something else. But six years ago when she'd applied for ninety odd jobs, this was the only one that accepted her. She knew she was being paid a pittance.

"The job market is changing again, there are more job opportunities out there. Your skill set's becoming more in demand. Come on, it's a dead end job. When was the last time you got a promotion or pay increase?"

"Don't remind me," Larissa grumbled.

"Well, just think about Gerald, the puppy running with his tail between his legs, and we'll catch up tonight, okay?"

"Yeah, can't wait. See you tonight."

"See ya hon'."

Larissa breathed out as she looked at the time on her cell. Time to head back to work.

Yay.

~∞~

4pm - Wednesday

Larissa had finished all the typing and was dealing with some filing. It was the first time in three weeks that she would finish and go home at a normal time. She whistled as she slotted the final file into the cabinet and turned to her computer. Trudy stood by her desk, a big smile plastered on her face.

"Paul would like another report done, just like the last one, but with more information this time."

"And?" Larissa could feel her smile fading from her face, and knew what was coming.

"Would you mind doing this, please, as a favour to me?" Trudy shrugged her shoulders, trying to pull her best little girl face as she handed the file across the desk to Larissa.

Larissa folded her arms across her chest, looked at the file and back at Trudy. She'd had enough!

For the first time in six years, clarity provided her with the insight she needed. Six years she had slaved her butt off. The late nights had been spasmodic to start with, but in the last six months, they had become more regular, until the last two months. Nearly every work night, Larissa had been at the office late to catch Trudy up on *her* paperwork – and without any recognition, or acknowledgement.

"You owe me too many favours."

"Yeah, but I know how much you like doing these."

"Whatever gives you that idea? You never thank me."

"Oh, I'm sorry, you do such an awesome job, I just assumed you knew that I appreciated it."

"You don't appreciate that *I* stay until eight nearly every night doing *your* work! "

"Oh well, thank you for staying late and doing these reports."

Larissa rolled her eyes, still ignoring the files that Trudy was trying to pass to her. "Nope, I'm drawing the line. You need to start doing your own work."

"I do plenty of work as it is, without having this to do as well." Trudy's voice sounded edgy.

"And I don't? Excuse me, but I do all of my own, plus half of yours. About time you did your own."

"Pardon? I do my own work thank you very much."

"Really? That's why I've been here until at least eight doing your reports and typing, while you head home, every day at five, religiously. I could set my watch by how fast you exit your office."

"How dare you speak to me like that."

"Me? What, telling you the truth? Paul doesn't even know that I've done those reports, does he?"

Trudy looked suitably ashamed as her cheeks flushed. She decided to change tack: "This is good training for you. You could get a promotion or pay rise if you keep up this good work." Trudy's smug smile didn't last long.

"And have you take all the credit? I don't think so. I've been here for six years, and not once have I asked for a pay rise. I'm a qualified legal executive, not a flippin' typist! I can't do this anymore, I've had enough!"

"Wh- Pa- How dare you!" Trudy's eyes narrowed and screwed up her face so much she looked like a badly imitated painting of Picasso's masterpiece.

"Oh, I dare. After the evening I had last night, I say bring it on!"

"I'll have you censured for insubordination!"

"What have I done that isn't the truth? You could try, but you know what? I've had enough, you conniving bitch. I quit!"

10

Larissa bent over, picked up her purse and started grabbing her personal effects from her desk.

"You can't quit!"

Larissa looked up at Trudy, her eyes wide as she waited for the reason.

"You need to do this report first!" Beads of sweat were starting to form on Trudy's forehead and her hands were shaking.

"Sorry, I can't. I don't work here anymore." Larissa said as she turned off her computer. She waved at Trudy before heading out of the door and down the hall to the stairs, slowly descending, trying to see the steps through her blurring vision.

What the hell had she just done?

Hell, quit her job.

Not that it was a good job.

But it was an income.

Now she didn't have any.

Tears fell down her cheeks.

Chapter Three

3am - Wednesday, London, England

Harley Orion knocked on the door again, trying to make it loud enough to wake up Nigel, without waking up the neighbours. He looked at the time on his cell and closed his eyes.

Three am.

Whoops.

But it was urgent. He was about to ring Nigel's cell when he heard footsteps coming to the door.

"Better be fuckin' good," Nigel said as he peered, bleary eyed at Harley through the narrow opening, the chain pulled tautly.

"Can I come in?" Harley hissed looking over his shoulder down the corridor.

Nigel didn't respond, just pushed the door shut, but Harley could hear the chain rattling and the door opened, allowing him to enter. He closed the door behind him and turned to his friend. Nigel yawned, looking at Harley as he continued to pace around the small entranceway.

"Let's go to my office," he said.

"Yeah," Harley replied, a hand running through his hair, a piece flopped over onto his forehead, but he didn't care.

"What's wrong?" Nigel asked as he flicked on the small lamp that lit up his tidy desk. He sat in the leather chair and waited for Harley to settle himself into the chair opposite, but he was too agitated.

"She's gone and done it, that bitch, she's done it. I can't believe it! Lying little bitch."

"Slow down, Harley, what are you talking about?"

"Brigette!" Harley's eyes were wide as he explained to his best mate what his on/off girlfriend had been up to.

"Rape? She's accusing you of rape?"

"I swear Nige, I didn't touch her, she came home in a hell of a state, clothing all messed up, black eye. When I asked her what happened, she got all lippy, so I grabbed her..."

"You grabbed her?" Nigel blew out a breath.

"Let me finish. I grabbed her and shook her. I could smell alcohol on her; she was fucking out getting drunk. I shook her..."

"Shook her. Mmm huh."

"Nige! Listen to me! She's accusing me of beating her up and raping her!"

"If it isn't your fault, then you don't have anything to worry about."

"Nigel! She called the cops on me last week for yelling at her and told them I had assaulted her! They will have me locked up in prison faster than you can kiss my arse! The paps are already commenting on all the bruises she seems to turn up with, the black eye from walking into the door last month, the bruises on the top of her thighs from slipping off the table at Tabuki's, she's a walking disaster zone, and I'm getting the blame."

"Shit, Harley. You get yourself in some messes don't you."

"Nige, please, you believe me don't you?"

"Of course I do. Who tried to warn you about Ms. Preston, six months ago?"

"I know, I know. Should have listened to you, but... anyway, what can I do? We had sex this afternoon, the cops will find my 'body fluids' in her."

"Yeah, and the fluids of the man she's been with."

"But what if they don't? I'm the one that's going to be accused of beating her up. Nige, I need your help. I gotta get out of here until this cools down."

"Are you sure you don't want to stay and face the music?"

"What music? I didn't do anything wrong."

"That's what I mean. Piers can make it right, just stay and tell the police what really happened."

"You know what the cops are like. They'd believe her over me anytime. Besides Nige, what about that incident at school?" He blew out his breath, trying to find a solution that would make all parties look good, but that wouldn't happen.

"You weren't charged then."

"No, the charges were dropped, but it will be in their system. I gotta get out of here."

Nigel sighed. "Okay, I have a mate that's just bought a property in New Zealand."

"New Zealand? Yeah, that sounds far enough away."

"You have to lay low though, no making appearances or showing your face around. Or Interpol will nab you, understand?"

"I'm not a child, Nige, I know what to do. Do you think I want to have my face splashed all over the papers?"

"Hey, any publicity is good publicity, right?" Nigel picked up the phone and started dialling.

Harley shot him a glare, he didn't agree. While his body was covered in tatts, and he was a blockbuster action hero, he didn't want any bad publicity, his record had been squeaky clean until his relationship with Brigette Preston, the blond haired, long-limbed temptress of trouble. He often woke up wondering what he saw in her until he saw her naked in his bed, then he remembered.

The sex was hot.

But other than that, they had no real relationship.

Certainly not one he would openly discuss with his parents. They didn't like Brigette, had made that very plain the first time he took her home to their estate just outside of London. His mother had tried to be accommodating, but Brigette, with her American accent, had declared the place 'quaint' and 'pretty', much to his father's disgust. He valued his parent's opinion, but for some reason, he didn't listen to them as far as Brigette was concerned.

Damn, why hadn't he listened to them?

Why hadn't he listened to Nigel? Nige was his oldest mate, having met at primary school, they had gone right through the schooling system together, except Nigel had gone to St Andrews University to study economics and management, while Harley had used his good looks to get into the theatre and eventually television and into the movies.

"Thanks Simon, yes, will do... Much appreciated... Bye." Nigel hung up the phone.

"That's sorted. Simon said it's going into winter over there, and the Lodge has closed for the season, so you can stay there for as long as you like."

"Where in New Zealand, is this lodge?"

"Just out of Nelson, in Abel Tasman National Park, or somewhere like that."

Harley hadn't heard of the place, but he could google it. "Okay, so how am I getting there?"

"The jet is ready at the airport, they'll fly you to Paris, and then across to Singapore, where you will get onto a commercial flight under the name, your real name, Jeremy Ryder. Here's your passport, go."

"But, clothes? Work?"

"Here's some cash, don't use your credit card, in fact..." he held out his hand, "leave it here with me. I'll wire some money to you in Nelson. Simon 'll make sure you get it. As for work, I'll tell Derek that you're sick at the moment, and taking some time out in France to recover. He'll understand. I've rung and there's a driver about to arrive downstairs."

"Okay, thanks Nige," he hugged his buddy and whacked him on the back. He picked up his passport from the desk and looked back at him.

"You're the best mate."

"Nope. Your best mate would make you stay and talk to the police."

Harley stared at him and shrugged. He couldn't talk to the police. Brigette had called them. Enough that they were starting to think that he was an abusive partner. That was the furthest from the truth.

15

"I can't."

"I know, now go." Nigel concealed a yawn, making Harley aware of the fact that it was closer to four am now, and he hadn't slept for the last 24 hours. He walked down the white carpet in the hallway and out the apartment door and made his way to the elevator. As the door closed, he leaned against the back wall and let the falling sensation overtake him.

It kind of felt like his life; how chaotic it had gotten.

At least Nige believed him.

He hoped.

The door opened into the crystal lobby of the apartment building. He walked to the door and peered out through the frosted glass. Sure enough, a driver had arrived with a small black sedan, not the limo he normally got. Thank goodness for discretion.

He looked left and right, making sure there were no cop cars around, and dashed out to the car.

"Hello Mr Orion, the airport?"

"Yes thanks," he said as he buckled his seatbelt, clutching his passport to his chest, he slowly allowed himself to relax.

Once he got to France, then he would be able to breathe a little easier.

Chapter Four

4:30pm - Wednesday, Nelson, New Zealand

Wiping tears from her face, Larissa opened her flat door and dropped her bag on the floor. She dragged her feet as she went into the lounge, wanting to crash out on the couch. Instead, she went to the fridge, but it was empty. She'd looked in there the day before and it hadn't changed, stale cheese, beer, diet coke, milk. She didn't even like diet coke, but she hated beer more, so diet coke it was. Popping open the can, she poured it into the only clean glass left in the cupboard. She looked at the dishes in the sink and the bench, wishing that the cleaning fairy had called in overnight. But obviously, it was way too busy.

She went out to the couch and sat down, pulling her phone out of her pocket and resting it on the arm rest. She had just settled onto the couch when there was a knock at the door. She sighed heavily and cast her eye at the time. Nearly five pm.

"If that's you, Gerald, you can forget it."

"It's not Gerald," said a vaguely familiar voice. She hurried to the door and opened it, wondering who it was. Her eyes opened wide and she smiled as she saw her landlord standing on the doorstep.

"Hello Mr Whelan, what can I do for you today?"

Mr Whelan stared sternly at her over the rim of his glasses. "You can explain why you have remained behind in the rent even after asking for you and Gerald to catch up?"

Her eyebrows drew together, a notch pulling between her eyes where a dull thud was starting. Her face felt cold with the news.

"Um, I'm not sure what you're talking about, would you like to come in?"

"I think it's best I do. I have spoken to Gerald several times over the last couple of weeks about the rent not being paid, yet you still haven't tried to make any back payments, let alone, attempt to reinstate the payments."

Larissa's heart rate increased, and she wiped her hands against her skirt. "I don't understand. The payments come out of the bank account each week, have been since I moved in two years ago. And why were you discussing it with Gerald and not me?"

"Gerald has been here every time I needed to talk to you, and he promised that he had spoken to you. I've also sent letters, there are copies of these in this file." He held up a manila folder, which had a pile of documents in it. It was quite a thick file, obviously, he'd sent a few letters.

"Can I read one of the letters?" She held her hand out, and it shook slightly.

"Yes." Mr Whelan handed her the top letter, dated ten days earlier. Her gaze flicked over the letter, stating that due to previous attempts to contact her, and her lack of response if she didn't contact Mr Whelan within seven working days, he was within his rights to issue her with an eviction notice. If she wanted to avoid such a matter, then she was to contact him forthwith.

"And Gerald... he said what exactly?" She handed the letter back to Mr Whelan. She couldn't believe this was happening.

"He said that he had spoken to you about it, but that you'd laughed it off and told him not to worry about it, that you'd taken care of it."

"He did, did he?" She put her hands on her hips as she considered him lying and wondered what had happened to the money. "I'm very sorry Mr Whelan, I will get onto it for you straight away, and get the arrears paid as well. How many payments have I missed?"

"Twelve payments, you haven't paid rent for nearly 3 months."

"What? Three months? How could that have happened, I would have known if the payments hadn't been going out."

"That's not the worst of it, here." He handed her a piece of paper. She cast her eye over the top of the page, she drew in a sharp breath and tears blurred her vision.

"An eviction notice? But Mr Whelan…"

"Look, Larissa, you've been a great tenant, but missing rent payments for three months without trying to make arrears, I can't afford that. You have 90 days."

Larissa looked down at the piece of paper in her hand. "I'll work on paying you the back payment of rent." She muttered.

"I would appreciate that Larissa. I understand that this is a shock to you, and I'm sorry. I hope things work out for you."

"Yeah," she replied, still trying to understand exactly what was going on.

"I'll let myself out."

"Okay."

"Oh, and I expect the rubbish around the side of the house to be removed too before you vacate the premises." He pointed to the window through which she had thrown the television.

She nodded, too scared to use her voice in case it cracked. She sat down heavily on the couch as she heard the front door quietly close. She closed her eyes and pinched her nose with her fingers, trying to hold off the sobs.

Who had I pissed off to get this treatment? Who did I anger? What god out there doesn't like me?

First Gerald, although that was well overdue. Then her job, as stupid and dull as it was, it was still money coming in. Now - no rent? No flat?

She jumped onto her laptop and pulled up the bank statement for the house account. Sure enough, money had been going into her account from her everyday account, but it was disappearing out the same day to - Gerald's bank account. She went back through the records and found that he had been fleecing her out of money for the last eighteen months, about the same time he lost his job. She clenched her fists, her fingernails biting into the flesh of her palms. Heat seared through her, making her face feel hot. Coming back to the most recent bank transactions, she noted that he had taken money out of the account the previous day, and she wondered if it was before or after she had chucked him out.

Immediately she changed the password to her account and planned to close it the next day. She looked at her laptop and wondered how he had managed to get the account password. Going online, she searched through, found an article and checked her machine.

There it was, a small keylogging program that he must have installed. He had access to all her account information. A small sob escaped her as she realised that he had password details for her personal bank account, savings account, all her social media identities. She considered throwing the laptop onto the ground, but she didn't want to have to buy a new laptop as well!

She closed the lid, and had a shower, deciding to get out and over to Julie's before she was struck by lightning or something as strange happened to her.

Chapter Five

The wooden door with a gold number 6 appeared from out of the cream coloured hallway, as if by magic. But Larissa knew it wasn't. Her feet had automatically walked her to Julie's apartment.

Since her discussion with Mr Whelan, the landlord, she couldn't get her head to function much past going to Julie's. She knocked on the door and waited, shifting from one foot to the other until her friend opened the door. The instant it did, tears started streaming down her cheeks, her eyes blurring, her ears ringing. She fell into her friend's open arms, and held onto her, as Julie dragged her through the door and onto the couch in the open plan, well-lit lounge room.

It was a few minutes before she felt safe enough to tell Julie what had happened, and Julie, sweetie that she was, knew that she would open up and talk as soon as she was able.

"Okay, so it's not just Gerald now, is it?"

"No," Larissa hiccupped, trying to take a deep breath to settle herself enough to open up and talk.

"Just wait a minute okay. You compose yourself and I'll get us a wine."

Larissa smiled weakly as she looked at her friend. She grabbed a tissue from the box that sat on the empty coffee table, and blew her nose, wiping at her tired eyes. All the tears had made them heavy and swollen, and she wanted to sleep more than anything else in the world. But first, she had to talk to Julie.

A wine glass with a pale liquid sloshing around appeared in her view. She held out her hand and Julie placed the glass within her grip. "Just sip it quietly," Julie suggested.

Larissa felt like giggling but snorted instead, making both girls dissolve into giggles.

"Okay, spill, what happened."

"After I spoke to you at lunchtime, I quit work."

"What? I didn't mean for you to quit without finding another job first."

"I know, but I didn't really have a choice. I got sick of being used. Trudy wanted me to do another report, and I've spent weeks doing late nights to supposedly catch everyone else up, except my work was getting further behind, and to top it all off, the boss thought the last report was excellent but doesn't know that I did it."

"Why didn't you tell him?"

"Who? Phil, or is it Pierce, or Perry, or Peter... hang on... it's... Paul!" She said, knowing that Julie would get the joke.

"Right, that explains that then."

"And I wouldn't trust Trudy to not say that I was just jealous of her or something.

Anyway, doesn't matter, I'm out of there now. She can look incompetent on her own, without me protecting her from herself."

"I like your thinking." Julie held up her wine glass, and Larissa clinked her own against it, before taking a mouthful. The lovely crisp fruity freshness filled her mouth and relieved a small part of her thirst. She took another large mouthful.

"So I get home, and my landlord is there, and serves me with an eviction notice."

"Oh?" Julie replied.

"Because of unpaid rent."

"What? How the hell did that happen? I know you, you would have that covered every week."

"I did, but apparently, Gerald's need was greater than a roof over our heads."

"But doesn't the landlord have to send you a warning notice?"

"He did. And he visited, and because he must have to keep striking it when I wasn't at home, he got Gerald, who told him that I was fixing the problem... when I actually didn't even know we had a problem!"

"Can't you offer to pay your landlord back?"

"I have, but he has every right to ask me to leave." She took another mouthful of wine, the tears threatening to fall again. She tried to steel herself against the agony that the last twenty-four hours had brought. "What am I going to do?"

"Shit, I don't know! You can come and stay here, but only temporarily - the office is available, but this place isn't big enough for the two of us."

"I know, Jules," she smiled weakly at her, as she swirled the wine around the glass. "Thanks for the offer, I'll see what I can do, but because of the unpaid rent, it's going to be hard to find somewhere else, especially if they use the Tenancy Tribunal for reference."

"Don't worry, we'll get you sorted out."

Both girls swallowed the last of the wine in their glasses, looked at each other and started giggling.

"Another one?"

"Hell yeah," Larissa replied.

~∞~

"Okay Laaree, you can move in here, just tell me when an' I'll clean ou' tha' room for ya."

"Thanks, Julesh, I appreciate it. You're such a good friend."

"I know. Where woul' you be withou' me?"

"Up shit creek, without a paddle man!" Larissa giggled as she leaned forward, banging her head against Julie's in an attempt to hug her friend.

"Okay, so once you move in, we gonna ge' you a job, at my firm," Julie said, blinking rapidly as she spoke.

"I don' know about that. We'll see, aye."

"Okay, but wha' you wanna do with yourself? You go' a grea' ott... opt... opptornuty... chance to star' again."

"I know, right! I dunno. Might do a tramp, you know, something I've always wanna do, aye."

"Tramp? As in walk with a pack on your back? Wow, where you wanna do tha'?"

"Yeah, thinkin' of the Abel Tas... Tasman."

Julie's eyes opened wide. "Cool, tha' woul' be so awesome."

"I know, right! So, might go and do that before I find a new job."

"Oh, that soun's like fun. Min' if I come along?"

"No, would be cool if you did." Larissa found herself blinking fast, trying to get the three images of Julie to come together, unsure which one to watch. Not only that but when she closed her eyes, the world would go faster.

Damn it. I'm drunk, she giggled.

"Wha's funny?" Julie asked, lying down on the couch, resting her head in Larissa's lap.

"I'm drunk." The giggles got too much, and she snorted as she laughed.

"Fuck yeah, an' its Wenes... Wedes... the middle of the week." Julie giggled. "Oh shi', I have work tomorrow." She groaned, closing her eyes. She opened them and Larissa watched Julie's eyes as they staggered around her eye-sockets.

"Better have some water, and go to bed," Larissa said, waving an unsteady finger at her friend. Julie started giggling again as she tried to get up, falling onto the floor in a laughing heap beside the couch.

"You crash here, aye," Julie said.

"I ain't drivin'," Larissa said, clinking her wine glass against Julie's, only she misjudged and the two glasses smashed, splintering glass over the floor and spilling wine over Julie.

"Be' time." Julie chuckled, plucking at pieces of glass, small bits of blood smearing her fingers.

"Off you go," Larissa said, trying to pick Julie up off the floor. They dissolved into a heap of giggles once more, as they headed off to crash out on Julie's king sized bed.

Chapter Six

Sunlight pierced her eyelids and she blinked them open. A sharp pain seared through her head and Larissa closed her eyes again, wishing the dull thud in her temples would go away. She opened and closed her mouth. It was drier than a desert and felt just as gritty. Larissa sat up on the couch and groaned as the pounding in her head increased with the upward momentum. Glancing at her watch, she gasped when she saw it was nine thirty.

"Shit!" She scrambled for her handbag and cell phone, ready to call work and apologise when she remembered; she no longer had a job. Torn between relief and anxiety, she put her head in her hands, trying to reassure her head that it wasn't going to come loose from her body.

Looking around the lounge, she realised that she wasn't at home either, and slowly her evening with Julie filtered back in, the laughs they had, the promises they had made.

Larissa remembered her decision to no longer just accept things but to take the bull by the horns and face life head on.

That was rather ambitious she thought.

The decision to go tramping.

Her head gave a decided thud at that suggestion. She'd always wanted to give it a try, but never found the time. Perhaps now, while she had some time off, she could - just go and do it.

Again her head gave a rather nasty wallop as if her brain was trying to tell her to settle down and stop trying to do too much at once.

She got up and got a glass of water from the kitchen, sculling it, and letting dribbles of water slide down her chin. Her mouth felt better, but the headache remained. She searched through Julie's cupboards until she found the paracetamol and slipped a couple onto her hand, chucking them at the back of her throat and trying to fill the glass before she gagged on the slowly dissolving and disgusting taste of the tablets.

Washing them down, she started the jug and set about making a cup of coffee. While she waited for the jug to boil, once more the idea of going for a tramp sprang to the forefront of her mind.

What's stopping me? Besides a headache?

What she really needed to do was assess her situation. She was a qualified Legal Executive. She'd lived in Nelson her entire life.

Perhaps she should broaden her horizons? She had to move out of her flat, she had no job, no ties, other than her family.

With her coffee cup steaming, she sat back on the couch and looked around Julie's apartment. It was nice, tidy and contained, but only really big enough for one. She could stay a week, maybe two, before she would have to find something else. That's if she could find something else within Nelson. It was a tight work market. But there were always job opportunities in Wellington or Auckland.

The idea of leaving Nelson behind gave her a small thrill.

A small town girl making it in the big smoke.

All her short life, she'd often wondered why she'd never amounted to much, but now she realised, it was her own limitations that kept her back. When she had qualified as a Legal Executive, she thought she was on top of the world, but the firm she worked for, the partnership broke down, and she had to be let go. The only other job's for her qualifications had been in other centres, but she hadn't wanted to move six years ago. It was too far out of her comfort zone. Hell, being unemployed, unloved and unhoused was out of her comfort zone, but she was still alive.

Perhaps this year was her year. Maybe she should go tramping.

Picking up her cell phone she sent a text to Julie. She didn't hear the annoying "What Does the Fox say" tune Jules used as notification, so knew that her friend must have it with her at work.

Her own R2D2 whistle let her know Julie had responded.

[Tramping? Suuuuure.]

I'm Serious. Let's do it

[You mad?]

Nope

[You're using it to run away from your responsibilities]

Nope, wanna try something new. You keen?

No response. But her mind had been made up. Drinking the last gulp of coffee, she found her car keys in her bag. She rinsed the cup and left the apartment, making sure the door was locked behind her. If she wanted to go tramping, she would need some gear. And for that, she would need some money, and to get that, she needed to go to the bank to sort out her bank account.

She stood by the door of her car, her head just pounding enough to let her know that she had drunk a little too much last night. She looked at the car and put her keys back in her bag. It wasn't far to walk, she could walk to the bank and get things sorted. She'd drive her car later when she had eaten something and wasn't likely to still be over the limit.

~∞~

Harley squinted at the bright sunlight that greeted him as he stepped off the plane. It was a smaller airport, not one he was used to. Normally planes arrived, taxied around and the door opened onto a gangway, which you walked through to get to the terminal. Here, the plane landed and you walked down steps into the open.

He placed the hat on his head and pulled down the brim. It was autumn, nearly winter in New Zealand, but the sun shone rather brightly, and it was really screwing with his eyes. With the long haul flight from Paris to Singapore and the flight from Singapore to Auckland and then Auckland to here, he felt like he hadn't slept in days, 31 hours of flight time, five agonising hours waiting for planes. He yawned, stifling it behind his hand as he came into the shade of the airport's covered walkways.

He breathed out as he stepped into the building and looked around. It was a small airport, but there were lots of people around, and he felt self-conscious being on his own. He made his way past lots of hugging people and exited the building, surrounded by a pall of smoke. At that moment, he desperately wanted a cigarette, but he didn't have any.

Now, he had to wait for his bags. Hopefully, someone would arrive shortly. Nigel had texted him and told him that Simon would meet him off the plane, but he didn't recognise anyone, not that he expected to know what Simon looked like.

It seemed to take forever for the bags to arrive, towed on a trailer behind a funny looking ATV. Quite old fashioned for an airport.

He remained standing back as everyone fell upon the luggage trailers, desperately pulling their luggage and lugging it through the crowds of people and children. How no one got trampled surprised him.

Within moments, the melee had gone, so he got his own overnight bag, the sole one left. He hefted it over his shoulder as a tall, broad-shouldered Maori smiled at him.

"Jeremy?" he asked. Taken aback by the use of his old name, he realised that this was probably his contact.

"Simon?"

"Yeah mate, welcome to Sunny Nelson."

"Thanks." He mumbled.

"This way." Simon talked non-stop as they headed towards the parking between two large gardens. He keyed open the boot of a large SUV and Harley threw his bag inside and climbed into the passenger seat.

28

"You can tell me to shut up, you know. I understand it's been a long flight for you."

"Yes, it has."

Simon started the car and remained quiet as he drove them around in circles until they got to the exit and he pointed the car towards the main motorway.

"Gonna head to Mot, and from there, we'll take the boat out."

"Mot?"

"Sorry, Motueka."

"Oh." He sat back and closed his eyes, not really wanting to see much of the scenery. What he really needed was sleep.

Or peace and quiet.

Fortunately, Simon didn't talk for the remainder of the trip, just turned the stereo onto the local radio station and left the music playing down low. He appreciated the attempt at giving him some space.

He awoke with a start as the car was slowing to a halt. He looked out over a beautiful bay, a city in the distance, golden sands along the beach. This place was paradise.

"We're in Kaiteriteri," Simon announced.

"I thought we were going to Mot-chew-eeka?"

"Well, Kaiteriteri is actually only about 20 minutes out of Motueka, this is where the boat is."

Harley looked around, several launches and a couple of yachts were moored around the bay. Off to the south, flash houses flanked the bay, separated from the main beach by a small spit of native forest. He opened the car door. Behind them stood a large cafe, and a camping ground, which had a few caravans and tents, but looked mostly empty.

"Summer season's been and gone; this place is packed on New Years. In fact, they close it off because it gets too busy. Half of Christchurch comes here."

Harley nodded as he grabbed his bag from the back and looked at Simon.

"This way," Simon said, nodding his head. On the beach sat a small metal dinghy, it didn't look big enough for the two of them.

"Is this how we're getting there?" Harley asked.

"Hell no! We need a bigger vessel for that. That's my boat, out there." He pointed to a larger launch, bobbing in the slight rise and fall of the tide. "PlayTime" was written along the side of the boat. It was a wooden planked double-ender with sleek smooth lines. The cabin didn't sit too high up on the deck, making for a nice low line boat.

He looked over it as Simon pulled up alongside. He clambered on and tied the rope off for Simon, before being passed his bag and Simon climbed aboard. He unlocked the padlock on the cabin door and opened it, allowing Harley to enter.

Inside was a beautifully arranged area, the fo'c'sle compartment held some bunks, and there was a half pulled curtain only showing the bottom base of a bed. Between that and the door was a large galley complete with gas oven, gas cooker and fridge. A table with two bench seats finished off the other side of the cabin.

He put his bag on one of the bench seats and went outside to help Simon get the vessel ready to head to Awaroa Bay.

By the time he'd got out Simon had already tied off the dinghy to the mooring rope and untied the launch. She drifted, slowly rising and falling, but the view out over the bay was like looking at a polished mirror, and once more he was pleased he had a hat and put his glasses on. As tired as his body was, the air and the view were enough to keep him invigorated.

"All right then," Simon said, wiping his hands on an oily old towel. He went to a small alcove and pushed a button. The engine throbbed to life, sending a plume of black smoke into the air.

"Just when she starts, other than that, she runs sweet as. Shouldn't take us long to get up the bay," Simon said, "You can go and rest if you want."

"No, I'm fine up here," Harley said, attempting his first smile in 24 hours. He hadn't even smiled at the air hostesses who had fawned all over him. They hadn't called him by name, so he didn't know if they knew who he was or not, but he was handsome enough to attract attention.

Simon concentrated on moving the vessel around the point to the open sea of the Tasman Bay. He throttled the boat into a higher speed and they cruised up the coast, resplendent with golden sands, and beautiful blue seas. The water was crystal clear, and in some places, he was able to see the bottom, covered in rocks. Large areas of native bush tumbled down the hills right to the edge of the sea.

The tranquillity of the scene filled him with a sense of peace and calmness, something he hadn't felt for a while. He didn't know whether to be happy or sad about it. Part of him enjoyed the quiet, but he also missed the hustle and bustle of London, it was almost too quiet here. Birds called out and strange black birds with white tufts of feathers at their throats flitted around, and birds with fan-shaped tails twittered and chirped as they dove in and out of the bush. It was so different from the concrete buildings and pigeons from home that he got quite engrossed in watching out for more that it didn't take long for the boat to be slowing down. He looked over at Simon, then at where the boat was pointed, a small sand-spit on a beach.

"You going to park up on the beach?" He couldn't keep the shock out of his voice.

"Nope, but you're going to jump ashore while I tie up the boat." Simon's cheeky smile creased his eyes, which sparkled with mischief. Harley didn't mind, it sounded like a good idea. He grabbed his bag and headed to the front of the boat.

"Jump when you're ready," Simon commanded him. The golden sand didn't look too far away, so he pushed off from the bow and landed, one foot on the sand, one in the water. It slowly seeped into his shoe, but he wasn't upset by it. He shook his foot and could hear Simon chuckling as he put the vessel into reverse and moved over to a mooring. It didn't look like it would be long before it would be out of the water, as the tide flowed out, but the small sheltered estuary like bay would protect the boat. And it would re-float on the incoming tide. He moved along the beach to where Simon had taken the boat and waited onshore for him to arrive. With his jeans rolled up, and crocs on his feet, Simon strode through the tide like a god rising out of the water. The graceful moves of the Maori man struck Harley and he was envious, for the first time in his life, not to have the self-assured confidence that Simon obviously had. Even though he was an action movie star, it was acting. He didn't feel nearly the same self-assuredness.

"Right, bro?" Simon asked. Harley picked up his bag and nodded as they set off down the beach.

"Should have brought the quad down, sorry."

"Quad?"

"Four wheel motorbike, it's a bit of a hike to the Lodge."

"That's okay," Harley said as he walked in the soft gravelly sand. It wasn't like normal beaches with grey sand. This was yellow, hence the name, Golden Bay. It shimmered in the midday sun, glinting every now and again. He would get to have a better look at it from the shore.

He stifled a yawn. The fresh sea air was taking its toll, that, and the fact he hadn't slept in days. He stumbled and righted himself, only to hear Simon chuckle.

"Yip should have brought the quad. Don't worry, it's not too far. You'll be looking forward to a good sleep then."

"Hell yeah," Harley said, sighing softly.

"It's very quiet here, you'll love it."

"I'm liking what I see already." The shade of the bush covering the path was a blessed relief. While it was autumn, and the sea breeze contained a chill, the sun was still hot.

They stepped out into a clearing and Harley whistled. "Wow, wasn't what I was expecting."

Simon laughed. "Yeah, lodge normally means a building, a large one. This one is more extended in lots of different areas."

The entrance of the building looked out of place surrounded by native bush. "Welcome to Hideaway Lodge." He led him past the reception area and into a kitchen facility.

"Here's where we will keep the stores for you to survive, I'll come down once a week with fresh meat and veggies for you."

"Thanks," Harley mumbled. "Can you show me to my room please?" His eyes were struggling to stay open and he kept tripping over his own shadow.

"Sorry, yeah, follow me." Simon led him out the back door and down a path. "We have you in the first villa, so you have easy access to the main building."

"Thanks." He let the bag slip from his shoulder as Simon opened the door and stepped aside. The room was large, with an upstairs area. A large misshapen piece of wood was used as a feature of the room.

"I'll stick around until you wake up, got some maintenance to do anyway."

Harley nodded and smiled as he shut the door. He walked over to the bed and sat down heavily. It was firm, just how he liked it. He unlaced his boots and swung his feet up onto the bed.

Bliss...

Chapter Seven

Julie had been less than helpful. She'd chickened out of the tramp, much to Larissa's annoyance, but the more Julie whined about Larissa going, the more she was pleased Jules was staying at home.

It had been ages since she'd stepped out of her comfort zone. In fact, she couldn't remember the last time, she'd done it.

She'd been to Cash 'n' Trade and the sales lady had pointed out the difference between a male and female pack, picked out boots and other tramping equipment she would require. It had cost her a lot of her savings, but she needed this tramp. It would be her opportunity to solidify some plans for her future in Nelson or elsewhere.

The Internet had provided a large portion of the information she'd needed, and a visit to the local Department of Conservation office had netted the hut passes she would require. That was another large expense - she hoped it would be worth the cost.

On the bright May Saturday morning, she arrived at Kaiteriteri, looking forward with trepidation to the trip up the bay to Totaranui. Her nerves settled uneasily into her stomach, fluttering around like butterflies stuck in a jar. A slight southerly breeze cooled her, making her realise the full extent of her decision — she was going tramping.

Tramping!

She'd never attempted anything like it before!

What's possessing me to attempt such a thing!

34

The vessel pulled out of the bay and rounded the corner. The captain made announcements over the speaker, pointing out places of interest. He circled around Split Apple Rock and recited pieces of history about various points and houses. Larissa soon tuned out his voice and the dull drone of the motor, focusing only on breathing and calming the growing panic within her. It wasn't too late to turn back. She could just stay on the boat instead of getting off at Totaranui, but then she would have to face her problems back home.

~∞~

Early afternoon the vessel pulled up to Totaranui beach, the golden sands glistening in the late autumn sun. The temperature was warmer, even though the sea breeze remained chilly. She pulled her pack onto her back, regretting her decision to bring a kilo block of cheese. She strode across the gangplank and up the beach, refusing to glance backward in case she copped out and ran back up the ramp.

Being the only person disembarking at Totaranui made her feel like everyone was watching her. Best to just keep walking up the beach and onto the steps, taking her up over the dune and onto the Totaranui Domain.

The Department of Conservation building was closed, locked up for the weekend, so instead, she settled at a picnic table, sighing as she dropped her pack. Only five minutes with it on her back and her shoulders were screaming in agony. She made a quick lunch out of crackers and cheese and a drink of icy cold water, before settling the pack on her back and finding out which direction she needed to go in order to find the track. It didn't take long, it was all well signposted.

~∞~

The shade of the native bush was refreshingly cool, and she settled herself down to a steady pace. With her mp3 player on, she focused on the beat, to match her footsteps, choosing a playlist of rock songs to keep her moving forward. It didn't take long for the first hill to approach and half way up, sweat poured off her. Her hamstring and calf muscles screamed and her lungs heaved, seeking oxygen. She yawned as she pushed herself forward to the next bend in the track, resting in the shade to recover her breath.

The views out over the bay would have been spectacular if she hadn't been so focused on staying alive long enough to get to the top, but once she made it, she congratulated herself for accomplishing her first hurdle - and getting over it. She breathed out, gulping in long breaths as she set off down the other side, plunging into the cool dampness of the forest, then out onto the beach, trying to find the track that disappeared at the end of the beach. On careful examination, she found a metal handrail half way up a rock face and used that to access the track once more.

By the time she reached the last flat part, she was ready for a rest. Low tide was still an hour away so she took her time reaching the estuary. As it was a tidal crossing, she had to wait for low tide to make her way across the mudflats. She had specifically brought her crocs and was glad for it when she saw all the cockle shells. They could cut feet in minutes and with the slimy mud, would easily get infected.

There were two other trampers waiting, and from the looks of it, they'd been there a while. She got out her map and looked over her progress, pleased that she had made it this far. Only about half an hour to three-quarters of an hour to cross the tidal flats and she would be at her first hut. Not bad for a four-hour walk. Her shoulders hurt from the pack, but once it came off, the ache deep in her shoulders eased.

She left her pack and read the information kiosks advising of the dangers of the crossing and to keep to the track. Larissa couldn't help but snort at that.

She glanced at her watch, the tide was down to a few channels of water, and she wondered if they would all go, or if she would still have to get wet. Slipping her crocs on and tying her shoes to her pack, she hefted it onto her shoulders and set off. The mud was firm underfoot, surprising her. She looked up and aligned herself with the large orange spot on the other side of the estuary, then strode across the sandy mud, judging the distance to the first water channel. The other trampers, plus one other, set off, following her. They hadn't had the foresight to take crocs or water booties, so had taken off their shoes and socks and were walking gingerly across the mudflats. She waded into the first channel, gasping at the coolness of the water, but pushed on. Thankfully, the water didn't get any higher than her knees.

Looking up, she checked the orange marker and once more adjusted her angle. The next channel was also shallow, but the one after that was deeper, with the water creeping up her thighs. She was relieved when she got to the other side and realised that there were no more channels to cross, just puddles to navigate around.

As she walked off the beach and up onto the grass in front of the hut, relief flooded through her, making her eyes sting with tears.

She'd made it.

On...Her...Own!

No one had told her she couldn't do it, that she wouldn't make it.

Her only inhibitions were her own limitations, and she had managed to quieten that voice as she got further into the walk.

She pushed open the door of the hut and looked around. It was empty, and the room echoed with her footsteps. She went into the first room and was surprised to find it a large bunk room. She let her pack drop to the floor heavily and leaned against the wall, sliding down to the ground and resting her elbows on her knees. She blew out a breath and let the tears fall.

They weren't just relief, it was the whole situation she had found herself in, kicking Gerald out, losing her job and her flat. She shook her head as she considered the mess she would have to sort out when she got back. Paying the back rent, plus the rent for the next six weeks. money she didn't have, because she'd spent it on purchasing the pack and tramping equipment.

She pushed the thoughts aside, wiping the tears from her face with the back of her sleeve. She opened her pack, rummaging around for something to have for dinner.

Chapter Eight

Larissa woke with a start, staring at the wooden structure above her and wondering where she was. As she turned her head to the side, Larissa remembered that she lay in the bunkroom of the Awaroa Hut. A smile crossed her face as she realised that she had slept all night for the first time in ages; in fact, she couldn't remember the last time she'd slept through the night.

She unwrapped herself from her sleeping bag which was twisted around her and stretched, yawning loudly. No one else had bunked down with her in this room, although a couple stayed in the other room. The trampers she'd crossed the estuary with yesterday had continued on. The travellers in the next door room were waiting for the morning tide before heading towards Totaranui.

Her muscles weren't as sore as she'd expected them to be, and she quickly dressed in her tramping clothes, a thermal shirt with a bright orange t-shirt over the top, leggings and shorts. She laced up the boots on her feet and packed away her sleeping clothes into the pillowcase that she used to store her clothing, and doubled as her pillow.

The sun wasn't up yet, and when she went outside, a slight frost iced the ground. She shivered, pleased she'd brought her warm clothes. She went to the toilet and filled up her bottle of water from the outside tap, ready to make herself a cuppa while she ate her breakfast. It didn't take long for the kettle to boil and she made up her tea, ate her muesli bars and drank her breakfast supplement.

The sun rose slowly above the hill up behind the hut, promising a hot day. It would only take four to five hours to walk to the next hut on the track, so if she left at eight am, it would be early afternoon when she arrived at the Bark Bay hut, but that didn't worry her. Better to get there early and set herself up, than late and not have a bunk at all, which probably wouldn't be such a problem considering the number of empty bunks at this hut.

~∞~

Harley put his cap on, pulled his sunglasses over his eyes and headed around to the back of the property to climb up the Skyline track. It was steep, but it made him feel alive when the blood pumped around his body. He couldn't get his usual exercise, but this was just as good. He set a steady pace, letting his body sweat, his lungs fill and empty slowly as he rose above the lodge, onto the plateau behind it.

He sat on the bench seat, which overlooked the buildings and beyond, to the bay. Light sparkled off the water, blinding him if he looked directly at it. The slight breeze rippled the water surface and boats left white wakes behind them like snail trails.

He'd heard from Nigel, the police had been to visit him, and asked questions about his movements. So far Nigel had managed not to lie, but he hadn't been truthful either. It twisted his gut to know that he was putting his friend in a precarious position.

It was illegal to lie and impede a Police investigation, but he hadn't done it. He hadn't touched her.

How could one woman ruin his reputation so quickly? He'd never been one to hit a woman or push them to do something they didn't want to do. 'No' meant 'no' as far as he was concerned. But Brigette knew what to do to make him respond negatively. He'd yelled at her in public, reporters had managed to catch part of the conversation and twisted it in their report, claiming that he'd threatened to hit her.

As if.

He had told her that he understood why some women drove a man to violence. Words that he shouldn't have uttered, looking back on it.

And when she'd turned up with a black eye at the Charity event, and then winked when she'd told the reporters that she'd walked into the bedroom door, they took the wink to mean that he'd hit her, when in actual fact, being drunk, she *had* walked into the bedroom door, while trying to find the bathroom.

He shook his head, wondering how he had gotten mixed up with such a woman. She wasn't the type he normally went for. He liked quiet girls, not wannabe actresses, who kept to themselves.

He didn't like his life splashed across the tabloid pages, he valued his privacy, yet Brigette had thought that being with him would be her next step into the movies. There was no way that would happen if he had anything to do with it.

He sat back on the bench, enjoying the breeze as it played across his sweaty brow, allowing the coldness to bring him back to this moment. Looking out over the sea, he was miles away from the trouble and strife of his life left on the other side of the world.

~∞~

Larissa brushed her teeth, packed away her cooking gear and pulled her pack onto her back, ready to head out.

It didn't take long for her to heat up, and she hadn't even got halfway up the hill before she took her thermal top off. She looked out over the sparkling bay and took a deep breath. The salt air, tainted with damp leaf rot, and the slightly smoky smell of the overnight fires invigorated her. The hill wasn't as steep as the one she'd crossed yesterday, but it still made her puff and sweat profusely.

She wasn't fit, by any stretch of her imagination. But she pushed on.

Head down, her cap pulled low over her face, she trudged up the hill, careful to avoid the ruts carved out of the sandstone track by storms over the years.

The morning sun was in her eyes as she looked up, blinding her from anything else on the track.

"Morning," said a deliciously smooth English accent. Startled, she looked up, and misstepped, her foot going into one of the water gouges and twisted her ankle. She cried out in pain as she pitched forward, the weight of the pack pushing her onto her hands and knees, grazing them. Stunned, she pushed back, her hands stinging, and her knees numb with shock, but the agony that radiated from her ankle grew and surrounded her. She huffed out her breath, trying to ignore it.

"I'm so sorry," the voice said. A hand gently touched her shoulder. "Can I help you up?"

She shook her head, her voice not yet strong enough to say anything.

"Does it hurt?" At this she looked up, glaring at the face that swam before her, her vision blurring as she adjusted herself into a sitting position. With the sun behind the man, she was unable to see what he looked like, not that she cared. Her ankle was too tender to think about anything else. She brushed the dirt from her hands, carefully inspecting the grazes. She pushed herself up, trying to move the weight of the pack more centrally on her back. Carefully, taking a couple of pushes from the ground, she managed to get herself up onto her knees, careful to avoid the grazes, which wasn't as easy as she thought.

The stranger leaned towards her, his hands outstretched as she attempted to get to her feet. A hand reached out, holding her upright. She hopped on the steep incline, trying to gain her balance.

"Easy there," the voice said. She turned to look at it and took a deep breath in, holding it. Her heart flip-flopped in her chest at the gorgeousness that stood before her. A handsome face complemented the voice. Hazel eyes shone brightly, and this close she could see a deeper green around the outer edge of the iris. Full lips curved in a slight smile, his face bristly with a few days growth, but it didn't detract from his handsome features. His sandy coloured hair fell over his forehead and sat just on his collar.

So captivated by his face, she put her foot down and moved her weight onto it. The pain raced up her leg. She cried out as she hobbled off to the side of the track, Mr Handsome beside her, holding her upright and assisting her to sit on a most uncomfortable rock. He crouched down in front of her.

"I'm so sorry, I didn't mean to scare you."

"It's okay, I should've been watching where I was going."

"It's a steep walk, it's not like you can see much, not with your head down, and the pack balanced on your back like you did."

She nodded, attempting to reach around for her water bottle. He unclipped it from the pack and passed it to her.

The cold water sated her thirst, and she poured some onto her ankle, hoping it would settle down, but she could already feel the swelling and bruising putting pressure on her boot.

"Damn," she muttered.

"Just sit and relax. Enjoy the scenery, that's what I was doing before your... arrival."

"Yes, it is nice," she said through clenched teeth, trying to tamp down the tears and the pain that pulsed up her leg. That and his small talk was starting to grate on her nerves. She just wanted it to be quiet, to allow the pain to ease in silence.

"I'm... Har... My name is Jeremy."

"Hi Jeremy," she said, wishing he would leave her alone.

"And you are?" He pressed.

"Larissa."

"Larissa, what a beautiful name." The sound of it on his tongue and the accent made her name sound exotic, but the velvet tones weren't penetrating through the fog that was gathering in her brain. The longer she waited, the more she knew her tramp was over. She wouldn't be able to finish with her ankle the way it was.

And the idea of walking down to the beach made the throbbing double.

Chapter Nine

Harley looked at the woman who sat on the edge of the track, her face pale and her winces of pain pulling at his gut. When she had turned to look at him, he couldn't help but feel a fluttering in his chest. He stilled momentarily as he took in as much as he could...as quickly as he could.

She would be stunning in normal circumstances. She was gorgeous, but the pain must have been pretty intense, the notch between her eyebrows deepened with each breath.

"You're not going to be able to walk, are you." Even his voice sounded stupid. She turned her head to look him in the eyes, her dark blue eyes mesmerising, the centre lighter than the outside. The look on her face told him what he already knew. Stupid question.

"I'll carry you down to the lodge," he said.

"It's all right, I have an epirb." She lifted the device on the rope around her neck and plucked it out from the inside of her t-shirt.

He panicked, looking at the device in her hands. She was about to press the button when he jostled her. The small yellow box fell onto the ground, and he reached across to grab it, instead knocking it across the track and down the steep embankment.

"Damn, sorry. I'm a bit of a clutz," he said, although he blushed slightly at his lie. He couldn't have her getting the authorities out here. He couldn't risk them finding him.

"What the hell did you do that for?" she cried. He looked at her distraught face, the deep lines around her eyes and mouth. Her sensual mouth.

"I... I didn't mean to," he said, turning his head away from her. He could feel the tension coming from her bunched up muscles, whether from pain or irritation he didn't know.

"One way or another, you have to get down the hill." He turned to look at her as she rested her head on her hands, her shoulders rising and falling quickly.

"Are you all right?" He put his arm around her shoulder, but she shrugged it off.

"There's painkillers in the top pocket of the pack. Could you get them for me?" She hesitated for a moment. "Please?"

He scrambled for her discarded pack, which she leaned on, and opened the top pocket. There was a lot of stuff in there, a deck of cards, Harlequin Mills and Boon book, notebook, pencil. He kept pulling items out of the pocket, surprised that so much could be stored in it. Finally, he found a small zipped purse, which Larissa pointed at. He unzipped it and pulled a card out. She popped two tablets, swallowing them dry before taking a swig of water from her bottle. Her throat bobbed and she pulled a face as she managed to get them down.

"Right, how about getting you down."

"What's your problem?"

"I... What do you mean?"

"You seem to be in a hurry to get down the hill."

"I was thinking about you, getting ice for your ankle."

"Seems more like you want to get away."

"Definitely not," he answered. "I wouldn't leave a woman in distress."

She glared at him.

He sighed. "Either way, you have to get down to the beach or the Lodge, to get help. You can't stay up here."

"You could get my epirb," she said.

He stood up and looked over the edge of the path. "Um, that's not possible."

"Why not?" She went to move, but he indicated for her to stay.

"It's a steep drop and covered in scrub. There is no way I could get it without getting into trouble myself, and then who would help you?"

"I could ring for help."

"Good luck, no cell phone coverage out here!"

She lowered her head again, took a sip from her bottle and looked up at him.

"How far down the track is the lodge?"

"It's quite a way, I'd have to carry you."

"I doubt that. No way. You're not carrying me."

"How else do you propose getting down?" he smirked at her discomfort. She looked around, and back at her pack. She stood up, twisting around on her good foot, and attached her drink bottle to her pack, hoisting it onto her back, she staggered, but settled herself, balancing the pack, and then stepped forward. She didn't even get the weight on her foot before she stopped. Harley put his arm underneath hers, gripping her shoulder.

"Lean on me," he said, but she refused to walk.

"This isn't going to work," she said quietly. Tears shimmered in her eyes. Without thinking, he used the pad of his thumb to gently wipe them as they fell down her cheek. She looked up at him, desperation in her eyes. He could see that she didn't want him to carry her, but she didn't have a choice.

"I'll piggyback you," he said. She looked at the steep track, then at him, and he saw her throat work again. Her shoulders drooped as the realisation settled on her.

"Okay."

He waited a moment, until she calmed herself, then stooped down. She didn't jump, or climb up, just leaned onto his back. He scooped her legs up and stood, the extra weight pushing down on him immediately. He religiously did weight training, he had to, to keep his body looking action star hot, but the weight of her, and her pack was more than he was used to.

"Leave your pack behind," he struggled to say.

47

"No, I'm not leaving it." She said, trying to ease up on his shoulders, but instead, she unbalanced him, and he nearly toppled backwards.

"Sit still," he growled. He tried not to blow out his breath as he adjusted her into a more comfortable position, then started across the track, past the bench seat, and down the steps to the first steep section of the track.

Larissa remained quiet as he staggered, and she sat stiffly on his back, refusing to move. He stumbled a couple of times, but he maintained his feet and staggered under her weight. It seemed to take forever to make it to the bottom, but he was grateful when he did and settled her onto the ground so he could have a rest.

"Mind if I have some of your water?" he asked. She looked at him, and nodded, removing the pack from her back in much the same way he had let her down. He waited for her to unclip the bottle and sip from it herself before she handed it to him. He unscrewed the lid and held the bottle up, tipping it into his mouth without touching his lips. The water was cold and refreshing. He'd built up a sweat carrying her, even though it was downhill, the extra weight had been a long overdue workout. His back was wet with sweat, and he noticed that her t-shirt was damp too. But it wasn't see through, not like his white shirt. He didn't care though, as he saw her looking at his tattoos.

"Nice ink," she said. It wasn't exactly a conversation starter, but he would take it.

"Thanks, a work in progress."

"There's more?" she asked. He desperately wanted to lift his shirt to show her more, but that would be too pretentious.

"Yeah, more to come," he said. She sat quietly, the pain must have eased, as the notch between her eyebrows had lessened, but she still winced when she moved her foot, which seemed to spasm every now and again.

"Let's get going."

"Do you have to carry me?"

"You can't walk on that foot. The only other option is to leave you here."

"What about a car or quad?"

"Nope, don't have either." He leaned down towards her, holding out his hand. She shaded her eyes as she looked up at him, before taking his hand. He helped her to her feet then stooped down. Once more she leaned against him, and he lifted her up. On the flat, it wasn't quite so hard, but it still took him half an hour before he reached the door of the main reception hall. He leaned forward to open the door and carried her into the lounge area, squatting down in front of a couch. She slid off him, his skin warmed as her body moved against his. He helped her remove her pack and settled her down, placing pillows under her foot. She leaned forward to unlace her boot, but he pushed her back.

"Lie down, rest," he commanded as he took her foot and gently eased the laces off as much as he could before gripping the toe and the heel of the boot and pulling it off. She hissed as it slid off, and he placed her boot on the ground. The sock, a thick woollen one was easier to remove; it peeled back off her foot. Her ankle was twice the size it should be, in fact, her ankle and little toe were connected by one large mass of blue tissue. He winced as he looked at it. He'd seen injuries to ankles before, but this looked nasty.

Placing her foot on the pillow, he headed off to the kitchen. Grabbing a tea towel and some ice from the freezer, he crushed it up and wrapped it in the towel. He headed back to the lounge to find tears streaming down her face. He pressed the ice pack to her ankle as gently as he could, but a sob wracked her body and finally she gave way to her tears, allowing noises to filter out of her as she wailed. He sat with the ice pack held to her ankle. She winced at the coldness, hissing with pain. Something about her fragility pulled at him. He wanted to hug her, to comfort her, but he couldn't do both, and right now, her ankle needed the ice pack more than she needed the comfort. He could do that later.

"Do you want more painkillers?" he asked. She shook her head, still crying.

"Anything I can get you?"

Again she shook her head and it was then he noticed the colour of her hair. The tips were a dark reddy brown, while the roots were white blond. Her hair was obviously a natural blonde, it didn't look like a dye job, except for the tips which were darker as the strand went down. It was glossy and looked so soft, he wanted to touch it. It was the only thing he could think of.

He pushed a strand behind her ear as she sobbed.

Chapter Ten

"Hey," his voice was soft as his hand pushed a strand of hair off her face. She looked up into his hazel eyes. His face had softened, and he looked close to tears himself.

"Sorry," she mumbled, but was she really? It wasn't just the ankle that she was crying about, it was the whole situation that had happened that week.

A week? Surely not!

She couldn't control her sobs, so she let them out until she finally hiccupped the last few. Jeremy's face was right next to her cheek, his breath hot on her face, his forehead not quite touching.

He was so close. Her body heated up from the closeness, her gaze moving restlessly around his face, his lips, so damned close. His hand came up, once more his thumb grazed across her cheek, removing a remaining tear. His touch sent hot fissures crashing across her body.

His other hand scooped more hair away from her face before he cradled it, his fingers caressing her gently. His lips closed in, and she sighed as she met him, her lips opening to allow the kiss.

What happened was beautiful, gentle, soft, urgent and needy all rolled up into one hot kiss. But where had that come from?

She opened her eyes and pushed away from him. He fumbled backwards, his hands letting go of her face, and one rubbed the back of his neck.

"Sorry about that," he mumbled as he staggered to his feet and fled the room.

What had she said? That kiss was lovely, but... There was always a 'but'.

She didn't even know the guy. He'd made her trip up, and lost her epirb. She hoped that there was a phone here. It was a large property, she knew it was the Hideaway Lodge, a rather exclusive place that was well frequented by the well to do. Something she couldn't hope to afford. She looked around the homely room, the large fireplace that dominated the space, the couches and seat placement. It was cosy and warm and welcoming.

Her gut plunged as she realised that she didn't have a home to go back to. In fact, her house had never felt homely. It had become a place to sleep at night. That was all. When had she given up on having the finer things in life?

She heard Jeremy moving around in the kitchen. He didn't seem to be in a hurry to come back, but then the confusion on his face had really said a lot. Perhaps it was him and not her that had the problem?

But it was too soon. She'd just broken up with Gerald. Gah, compared to Jeremy, Gerald looked plain and dull and boring. Jeremy was buff, his muscles well defined. His shirt had gone opaque with sweat and she'd seen his tattoos, not that she could tell what they were, Gerald was too scared to get any done. She had an armband done in her early twenties, but never followed it up with anything else.

Jeremy was everything she wanted, physically, in a guy. So why had she backed off when he'd kissed her?

She pinched the bridge of her nose and closed her eyes. All the thinking had removed the ache from her ankle, but it did nothing for sorting out her problems... and instead seemed to create a headache.

"Do you want a drink?" Jeremy called from the kitchen. His voice didn't seem quite as friendly as it had moments before.

"Yes please, water would be nice," she called out, her voice cracked with choked emotion. She hoped he'd heard her; she didn't want to talk again.

A glass of water appeared beside her, and he walked away before she could respond.

"Thanks," she mumbled to his retreating back. She heard his footfalls on the tiles in the kitchen, then a door closing. Silence told her that he had left the room.

She took a large gulp of the cold water and wondered what god she had upset in a previous life.

~∞~

Harley breathed out and brushed his hand through his hair as he marched off to his room. What the hell had he been thinking?

He hadn't actually, his other member had been.

He rubbed it, trying to ease the ache as it slowly went down again. Never mind the fact that she pushed him away. At least she had the good sense to see it wasn't a great time.

Would any time be a good time?

He shook his head and opened the door to his room. All he really wanted to do was go for a run, let off some steam, something. He opted for a shower instead, turning it on and stripping off his shirt and long shorts before testing the temperature of the water. It wasn't quite warm enough, so he stared at his image in the mirror.

Why had she pushed him away? He didn't look that bad, did he?

In London or even LA, he had girls throwing themselves at him, yet here... not that he needed that complication right now.

He stripped off his boxers and climbed into the shower, letting the lukewarm water wash over him. It was cold enough to make him wake up, but warm enough for him to wash in. He stretched his muscles, his shoulders and lower back aching from carrying Larissa down the hill. Whatever possessed him to do that? He knew he couldn't let her activate her epirb; does that mean she is now his prisoner?

He shook his head before leaning against the cold tiles. *What have I done?*

They could call one of the boat operators, and get them to pick her up, but she really needed medical assistance. If the police should turn up, they would want to know who he was, or one of them might recognise him.

Damn. If only he hadn't gone for a walk that morning, if only she hadn't been on the track at that particular time. He could beat himself up all day. He would have to ring Nigel and see what he had to say, but he could almost hear him now. "Get rid of her, I don't care how you do it, just get her back to Nelson."

He washed his body and his hair, rinsing off the lather and waited another minute under the water. He turned the shower off and dried himself vigorously, before wrapping the towel around his middle. He went into the main bedroom and picked up his cell phone. It didn't work here, but it had his contact phone numbers on it, and he picked up the landline and dialled out.

Nigel picked up on the fourth ring.

"Hello Harley,"

"Hey Nige, how's it going?"

"Good. How are you doing in New Zealand?"

"Not too bad. Settled in, nice place this Hideaway Lodge."

"Simon keeps telling me to bring the Mrs."

"You have to, it's worth it."

"Okay, so what's up?"

Harley swallowed. Nigel knew him so well. "Nothing. Why does anything have to be up?"

"You wouldn't ring me at ten pm at night unless you were concerned about something."

"Well, ahh, yes, right. Okay, here's the thing-"

"Oh god, you got a girl. How the hell did you manage that?"

"Well, she tripped and damaged her ankle, and this place was the closest."

"Why didn't you let her set off her locator beacon or whatever it is that trampers carry?"

"Um... because I threw it off the track."

"What?" Harley shuddered as he heard the anger in Nigel's voice.

"I couldn't have half of the Nelson Police force coming out here to find me, could I?"

"Where is she now?"

"She's in the dining hall."

"Get the boat to pick her up."

"I can't, you see, there are lots of people on those boats, and someone is bound to recognise me."

"Yeah, I guess. The police called around here a week ago, wanting to know if I had seen or heard from you. Told them I hadn't seen you since Wednesday morning, I didn't tell them what time, and that we spoke about work, which we did, and that you left. I didn't lie, but I wasn't exactly truthful either."

"God Nige, I don't like other people being dragged in on my shit."

"Harley, it's what I'm here for. And as far as I can gather, from my sources, you are completely in the clear, but you're right, she has filed charges, and the police are actively looking for you. I don't think they've worked out that you're overseas yet, but once the media get the story, you can kiss the anonymity goodbye."

"Yes. Right. I need to get Larissa out of here as soon as possible. I'll arrange for a boat first thing in the morning then. Sweet."

"Right, call me tomorrow and let me know how you got on. Are you coping okay otherwise?"

"Yeah, I'm doing okay." He shrugged, knowing that he was lying to his best mate.

He wasn't okay.

He was a mess, and all because of a bloody woman. How did they manage to do that?

"Take care, Harley."

"Yip, you too Nige, catch ya later."

He hung up, not waiting for Nigel's response because he knew there wouldn't be one. Getting Larissa on a boat tomorrow was a good idea. While she still didn't know who he was, he could remain anonymous.

The best one yet.

He could just rug up and make out like he had a cold or something, that would explain a scarf, which he did bring, and his big jacket would hide his muscles and bulk. What was he worried about?

The world finding out that Harley Orion ran from his problems.

Chapter Eleven

Dressed in jeans and a long sleeved t-shirt, his hair swept off his forehead, he headed back to the lounge area, ready to face the music, because being a woman, no doubt, Larissa would be pissed at him for leaving her alone.

But he needn't have worried. She lay asleep on the couch, well, more perched on the couch. Her foot rested on a chair she'd pulled over, and the ice pack had left a puddle of water underneath her ankle. The television was on, with the sound down low. He crossed over, about to switch it off when he heard the news story that came up on the midday news.

"London Police confirm today that they are looking for Harley Orion, the action star, most famous for his role as Jack Rigger, the vigilante for hire in the Rigger movies. He is wanted in connection with a sexual assault on his girlfriend Brigette Preston," the news anchor announced.

Harley stilled and watched the rest of the report with a growing ball of coldness in his gut. "The Movie Gazette confirms that Preston has pressed charges of rape, but she refuses to confirm or deny that they are against Orion, only saying that he would be better off talking to the Police. They have spoken with his agent and manager, Nigel Hall, who refuses to pass comment on this matter at this time. The Police suspect that Orion has fled the country and are following up leads."

"Oh shit," Harley muttered. He scratched the back of his head and looked over at Larissa. She snorted and grunted but settled back into her sleep. Thank goodness she hadn't seen it.

With his picture all over the news in New Zealand, it wouldn't take long for people to recognise him if he went out onto the beach, or even flagged down the next water taxi that passed through the bay. He looked at Larissa, her eyelashes clumped in dampness, resting lightly on her cheek. They fluttered a little and her eyeball moved underneath her lid, but she didn't wake up. He'd have to keep her here until she was able to make it to the beach on her own. He couldn't risk going out and being seen. Nigel had warned him to keep a low profile.

He looked at his watch. If she slept for much longer, she would miss the next water taxi departure. He left the room, leaving the television on, figuring that if he turned it off, somehow it would wake her up, and he couldn't risk that. She needed to sleep for a while longer. Then he could explain that he would call for a water taxi to pick her up tomorrow. That allowed him another day to get this facial hair that little bit longer.

He went into the kitchen and started cooking himself some scrambled eggs for lunch, something he knew was quick and easy to make without creating too much mess. He put the coffee pot on and brewed up a nice strong coffee. Stirring in two sugars, and some milk, he sat at the stainless steel bench and ate his meal, keeping an ear out for any noises from the lounge.

She cried out at one stage but remained sleeping for most of the afternoon. He didn't want to wake her, but if he didn't, she would end up awake half of the night.

Around three in the afternoon, she woke up. He'd been watching a movie on the television when he noticed her head jerk up. Her focus was glazed as she looked around, her eyes trying to focus on the darkness in the room. The late afternoon sun streamed in through the reception door but didn't penetrate into the lounge.

"It's all right," he soothed, placing his hand on her arm. Goosebumps erupted over her skin at his touch and she looked down at it, then at him. She blinked and rubbed her eyes before a small smile peeked at the corners of her mouth.

"How's the ankle?" he whispered. He didn't know why.

She moved it, hissing in pain as she repositioned her leg on the chair. "Sore," she replied. He nodded.

"You've missed the last water taxi out of here, we could try again tomorrow."

She nodded, her blushed face brightening a little.

"More painkillers?" he asked. She nodded as she leaned forward to retrieve her forgotten glass of water. He brought the blister pack to her and let her take out as many as she needed, before putting it on the floor in front of her.

"Hungry?"

"Yeah, I am."

"Ah, she has a voice." He smiled at her reddening cheeks. "What would you like?"

Larissa ducked her head down, pushing an errant curl behind her ear. The action, endearing, and innocent, he wanted to take that curl into his own fingers and play with it.

"What do you have?"

"Pretty much anything you can think of."

"Salmon and anchovy pizza?" she asked. He wrinkled his nose at the combination. Salmon or anchovies on their own, but together. Urgh.

She laughed, a tinkling delightful sound, so different from the earlier tears. Her eyes were puffy with crying, but at least she was smiling now. It made her eyes sparkle with life.

"Do you like scrambled eggs?"

"Yeah, I do. With some ham? Please?"

"Coming up, madam," he stood and bowed to her. She giggled again, the sound like bells in the air, something light to listen to.

He bustled around in the kitchen before he stuck his head through the doorway. She looked up and saw him, and he pulled a face. The laughter was infectious, and he wanted to hear more of it. He found an apron and put it on, and sweeping his hair off his face, he served up her meal, balancing the plate on one hand, and tucked the other behind his back. He knelt down before her, gave her the plate and then produced the cutlery with a flourish.

The smile totally transformed her face; her eyes flashed a beautiful azure blue, the corner of her mouth dimpled, and there were laughter lines around her eyes. Her animated eyes captivated him.

All of her captivated him, but the eyes, when she laughed were beautiful.

He removed the apron and sat back, watching her devour her meal. Harley wanted to watch her for hours, but she kept looking up and him and his constant staring made her uncomfortable.

"Have I got something on my face?" she asked.

"No, sorry to stare, but you are very pretty."

Her cheeks blushed a dark red, and her eyes darkened, as if what he had said upset her.

She didn't look up at him again.

Chapter Twelve

He disappeared out into the kitchen and he heard the volume on the television increase, she was quiet as he made the cuppa's and listened to the program while he was gone.

It ended and a movie started.

An action comedy.

He recognised the starting music, and felt the skin on his face tighten and a knot tightens in his gut.

He placed her mug on the coffee table beside her, within her reach and settled on the couch, the cushion dipping and their thighs touching. A sliver of fire ran up his leg from where they touched. She looked over at him and smiled.

"He kinda looks like you," she said, looking at Harley Orion on the screen. He turned and looked at his younger self. He'd dyed his hair white blond and shaved it short for the role, and his face was a little rounder back then.

"You think?" he asked, hoping that wasn't a line from the movie.

"I have other movies we can watch," he said, hoping that she would say yes, but she shook her head.

"I like this one. It's funny, could do with a laugh."

He blew across his cup, trying to hide the trembling in his hands. He put the cup down instead and gripped his hands together in his lap.

"Relax," Larissa said, slapping his hands with her left one. She looked over at him, shock on her face from having touched him. He smiled, reached over and took her left hand in his. She allowed him to hold her hand in his lap. His thumb rubbed across the top of her knuckles.

He watched her as the movie progressed. She laughed, gasped, hid and giggled at all the right moments. She jumped when the bad guy crept up behind the hero and heroine and fired his gun. She looked at him, her eyes wide open.

"It's okay, it's only a movie."

She giggled nervously and he pulled her around until she was tucked up under his shoulder. She smiled up at him and turned her attention back to the movie.

The ending was coming, where the hero and heroine kiss in the helicopter, the wind whipping their hair about their faces. He looked down at her, and saw her eyes wide open, her mouth open, the tip of her tongue wiping across her bottom lip, moistening it. Her mouth closed, her lips plump and kissable.

He leaned forward, his right hand coming up to cup her face. She turned her head and looked at him, closed her eyes as he got closer, her mouth opening.

It was all the invitation he needed. He brought his lips to hers and kissed her. She sighed, a small noise at the back of her throat, and he wanted to lie on top of her right there and then, that sound fired a line of desire straight into his groin. He broke away, and she opened her eyes, wide with surprise at the kiss.

"I wasn't expecting that," she murmured. He smiled, and leaned in again, claiming her mouth in a more bruising and crushing kiss than before, his tongue moving along her lips, and she parted them, her own tongue exploring his mouth.

She leaned into him, her breasts pushed against his arm. He wanted, desperately, to reach up underneath her t-shirt and touch her, roll her nipples into tight tips, instead, he pushed her away, gently.

"I'm sorry," he muttered, turning his back to watch the television again. He felt her stare boring into his head, and he resisted the urge to check and see what she was thinking. He didn't want to see the annoyance or grimace on her face.

"I'll take you to your room," he muttered, pulling her to her feet. She was reluctant to leave, but he needed space, and he couldn't let her sleep on the couch again, it wasn't that comfortable. Darkness had fallen while they had watched the movie.

"I'm not ready-"

"It's late, and you need to rest your ankle."

"Tell me what-"

"I'm sorry. I shouldn't have imposed myself on you."

She stared at him for a moment, opened her mouth and closed it. She sat forward on the couch, ready to stand up. He slipped his arm under her armpit and across her shoulders. Her arm came across the back of his neck and he held it. Fissures of desire flood his system, but he pushed them aside. He helped her out the door and along to the room next to his. He opened the door and led her inside. Her head moved from side to side as she took in the room. He could tell she was impressed as her eyes opened wide and her mouth opened too.

He took her over to the bed and helped her sit down.

"Umm, everything should be here, towels are in the drawer in the bathroom." He backed towards the door. "I'm next door, that way," he said, indicating over his shoulder with his thumb. "See you in the morning." He closed the door so he didn't hear if she responded or not. He didn't want to know, he had already confused her, and himself.

Why had he kissed her?

Again?

Chapter Thirteen

Larissa tossed and turned during the night. Between the pain in her ankle and the storm that whipped up outside around midnight, she felt restless and unable to settle. The gale blew against the building, branches scratching at the windows reminding her of childhood nightmares and she cried out, burying her head under the blankets as lightning flashed followed by the bellow of thunder.

She whimpered as she moved her ankle, which she'd carefully packed with pillows, but they'd moved, and the weight of the blankets made it ache badly.

Sniffing back her tears, Larissa tried to remind herself she was an adult, but she'd woken to find herself in a foreign place, and the lightning streaking through the window had made her feel sick and childlike.

A pounding on her door made her scream at the same time it flung open, revealing rain in sheets and a figure backlit by a flash of lightning. Torchlight penetrated the room, illuminating her room as she huddled under the blankets, shivering. Her heart thumped loudly in her ears.

"Are you okay?" A gentle voice asked. She looked up, still only seeing a shadow. She pushed against it, knowing she was defenceless with her ankle.

"It's me... Jeremy."

"Jeremy?" Even to her, her voice sounded childlike.

He sat on the bed beside her, smoothing her messed up hair, the action was soothing and her breathing calmed down. His hand curved around her jaw, the whisper of touch sending thrills through her nerves and warming her up.

The next flash of lightning seared the look of concern on his face, as he gazed down at her. Something in her eyes must have disturbed him. He pushed her over in the bed and climbed in beside her.

She hesitated momentarily, but the rumble of thunder made her huddle in against him. His arm went around her, pulling her close to his side as she hid her face in the soft t-shirt he wore.

His scent, a combination of masculine pheromones and a musky aftershave with hints of pine, filled her nose and she inhaled. A soft jasmine scent told her that he used laundry powder to wash his clothes.

Somehow the scents comforted her, making her shivering and murmuring quieten down. Jeremy settled down into the bed with her, and her head ended up in the crook of his arm, her own arm draped across his chest. His fingers played up and down her arm, the hairs responding to the touch, tendrils of desire curling through her body.

"Why did you come in?" she asked.

"I heard you cry out. I'm right next door. I had a sister who didn't like storms, and this is what I used to do with her."

"Oh," Larissa responded, trying to ignore the way her body responded to his voice. She wanted to grind her hips into his side, the urge so strong she nearly did.

"I'm sorry about earlier," Jeremy said. Larissa's mind wasn't thinking straight.

"Earlier?"

"Yeah, the... ah, the kiss."

"It was perfect," she purred, into his chest.

"It was? I mean, I'm sorry I encroached on you like that, it's not like me to be so forward."

"Encroached?" Larissa couldn't stop the giggle that bubbled up within her.

"What's so funny?" He pushed her off as he attempted to see her face, but it was pitch black, she couldn't even make out the features on his face.

"Encroach. It's a rather old-fashioned word. Besides, you weren't encroaching. I would have pushed you away if I didn't want it," she said, inching her way back down so her chin rested on his chest.

"You wanted it?" His voice went husky.

"I didn't resist."

"Can I kiss you again?"

Her lips found his first, his tongue slipped into her mouth, and she trembled with the pent up desire that had coiled like a snake in the pit of her stomach. She wanted to climb on top of him, take him, but her ankle restricted her movements. He rolled her onto her back, and carefully positioned her leg so he didn't hurt it. Pinning her to the bed, he deepened the kiss, stealing her breath and her self-restraint as she felt his hardness at the base of her stomach.

Her hands reached up, tugging at his shirt, trying to pull it off his back.

"Please," she whispered into his mouth. She felt the jolt as the realisation hit him. She held onto him, preventing him from pulling back.

"Lari, I want you, I do, but... I can't do this." He eased her arms from around his back and rolled off her. The action and the coolness of his missing body chilled her.

"You can't?" A solid cold mass sat in the middle of her chest, about to explode into a million shards that would tear her body apart.

"It's complicated," he replied. She felt the bed move and the blankets pushed aside.

"You - you have a girlfriend?" She gulped back the words, feeling a coldness creep up her face.

"No, nothing like that - I can't tell you."

"You're... gay?"

"Heavens no! It's not that. You're gorgeous... Please, don't ask."

The bed moved as he stood up and paced across to the door.

"The worst of the storm appears to be over. I hope you sleep well." He opened the door and left.

She lay in the bed, stunned. Wondering what had happened. Why didn't he want to do anything? Kissing? Cuddling?

Was he allergic to relationships like so many other arseholes out there? A single tear trickled out from under her eyelid and left a wet trail down the side of her face. The cold mass shattered, and she felt alone, and for once in her life, unloved and unwanted.

How could one man, one she had just met, have her feeling hot and horny one minute, and totally undesirable the next?

What was it with him? His good looks and charm were cute, but he lacked something.

His eyes.

They were sad.

She hadn't thought about that before. His eyes were an insane blueish grey colour - unusual really, but in their depths, there was a sadness, a long-term sadness.

A determination to stay away from anything that remotely seemed like love.

Her heart broke all over again, for him this time. Something had happened that had scarred him, turned him away from love.

Another tear fell, and she sobbed as she cried for all the pain and hurt within the walls of the building.

Chapter Fourteen

Harley sat on his bed as the light finally came, at least an hour later than usual. He could hear the swell on the nearby beach, the remnants of last night's storm, which probably hadn't quite let up.

The wind had eased, but the rain persisted, and his room felt damp, although it was probably because he sat in the cold tee shirt and boxers he'd worn when he went through to Lari's room.

He hadn't gone in because he'd heard her, it had been pure instinct. His sister was petrified of storms, and he'd gone to check on Lari, to make sure she was all right, but seeing her huddled underneath the blankets and whimpering, he knew she needed him.

Whether the storm had upset her, or she'd had a nightmare, he didn't know, but he went to comfort her.

And then she'd cuddled into him.

It felt so nice having a woman snuggle up in his arms, her hair right underneath his nose, a rich strawberry smell taking over his senses. He'd let his hand brush up and down her arm, he'd felt the small, almost indefinite move against his hip, and then she'd kissed him.

She'd kissed him.

He closed his eyes, his body surging with the memory, his heart pounding.

Lari had felt good, smelt good, tasted good, so why had he turned her down? Why didn't he want to take it any further?

Because he didn't want her to get caught up in the mess that his life had become.

He heard the betrayal in her voice.

He'd hurt her, for the second time.

He slapped the palm of his hand onto his face.

How did he keep doing this?

She seemed like a really nice person.

Why did he keep hurting her?

Unintentionally of course.

But he kept hurting her - physically and emotionally so far. He hadn't seen the tears, he'd heard them in her voice. He knew what it sounded like, the bimbo always did it. When Brigette did it, it drove him crazy, yet from Lari, it was a sound of genuine pain. Recent pain.

When had he started calling Brigette, the Bimbo?

And when had he started calling Larissa, Lari?

He shook his head and walked to the bathroom for a quick cold shower. No matter what he told himself, his body betrayed him. He tried to put his morning arousal down to thinking about Lari and the kiss, but he knew he was kidding himself.

Harley sighed as the water sluiced down over his head and his face.

He so wanted to tell her, why he was there, why he couldn't touch her, why he couldn't *resist* touching her, but he knew that most women would freak out, and run. Not that Lari could run, but she would freak out.

He turned the shower off and grabbed his towel, roughly scrubbing at his hair and beard.

He hated facial hair. It was scratchy. He preferred a clean face unless of course, the role called for a beard, but most of the time it didn't. He desperately wanted to shave it off, but he couldn't risk Lari, or anyone, recognising him. There were six days of growth now, it was getting scruffy. And he hated looking anything less than immaculate.

He dressed in boxers, jeans, and black tee shirt, and pushed his hands through his hair, trying to pull it into some sense of order. The whole time, one ear was tuned into next door, to hear if Lari was awake and moving around. No doubt he would hear her, as she wouldn't be able to walk, only hobble or hop.

A loud bang next door jolted him into action and he ran to his door, throwing it open and rushing to Lari's room. He knocked and called through the door.

"Lari? Are you okay? Can I come in?"

There was a muffled shout, and then her voice. "Please, I need help!" He opened the door and stepped into the room. Her sheets were a crumpled mess, a hand waved above the far edge of the bed.

"Lari, are you okay?" He came around the end of the bed. Lying on the floor, tears on her face, lay Lari. The pain on her face pulled at his heart strings, and he wanted to wrap her up in his arms and comfort her.

"I forgot," she mumbled, holding out a hand to him. He took it and reached for her other one. With the greatest of care, he pulled her up onto her feet. He got to see that she wore a singlet top, and silky boxer briefs. His morning arousal stirred again. He couldn't help but look her up and down, appreciating her long lean legs, her small waist, firm breasts. His gaze moved over her restlessly, trying to find a fault, but he couldn't. No matter what, he couldn't find any wrong with her.

"Have you finished?" The angry tone disturbed him.

"Sorry," he stammered, letting go of both her hands and her arms wheeled to balance herself. He steadied her with one hand while trying to keep his distance.

"I... I want to apologise for last night."

"Again? You're always apologising."

"I'm sor..." he grinned. "Okay, I'm not sorry, I enjoyed it," the smile dropped from his face. "But we can't do anything, no matter how attractive I find you."

"You keep saying that too." Her tone was cold as she eased herself onto the bed.

"I've just broken up with someone. I don't want to be a rebound relationship if anything happened. IF. I want it to be something more, see where it goes."

"Rebound? I've just broken up with someone too. And I'm not the type of girl to bounce from bed to bed. But you're right. This would be totally wrong for *us.*"

Through the pain in her eyes, he could tell she was lying, just like she knew he was.

He had checked out of his relationship with the bimbo a long time ago, even if he'd stayed with her. He sighed.

"Why the sigh?" Lari asked him.

He shook his head, "Doesn't matter. Do you want a hand to the shower?" he looked towards the bathroom. Anything was better than looking down on her, down her shirt to the hint of breast he could see. He'd noticed that she must be cold, as her nipples had started showing through the singlet top. He realised what he said.

"Not that I will get in the shower with you!" The words gushed out of his mouth. "I meant, I could help you get into the shower, and out." He shut his eyes. That sounded worse.

"Yes, please," she held his arm for support. He stopped talking because he knew he would just screw it up even more.

He put his arm around her shoulders and stood behind her, holding her like they were about to dance. Having her that close, the scent of her body and hair, went straight up his nose. He tried not to sniff too loudly. She hopped her way into the bathroom and he set her down on the toilet seat while he turned on the shower. A plastic stool sat in front of the vanity, so he put that in the shower. She didn't even need to ask, as he left the bathroom and returned with her pack for her to pull out her toiletries and clothes.

"Think you can manage from there?"

Lari looked around the bathroom and back to him. It was small enough space for her to hop around and use the edge of the shower stall to balance herself. The bathroom had a tile floor, which went straight into the shower cubicle so no lip for her to have to climb over. The tiles had a slightly textured surface, so no chance she could slip. He looked once more around the room, checking that she would be okay.

"I'll stay out here in case you need me," he said, leaving as steam started to fill the bathroom. He leaned against the door, wondering how he had managed to stay so composed. All he wanted to do was let his hands explore her all over. He shook his head, trying to dislodge the thoughts that were sending thrills throughout his body.

Chapter Fifteen

Larissa sat in the shower, trying to make sense of what was going on. Jeremy was worse than a leaking tap! Sometimes it stops, sometimes it doesn't. While society dictated that she should wait to start a new relationship, she couldn't help but feel an attraction to Jeremy. He was taller than her, his touch was gentle and warm. His lips... oh, his lips were stuff legends were made of. Such full, biteable lips. Soft, yet demanding. Everything about him was contradictions.

She sighed and started lathering up the soap, hoping to wash away the frustrations she felt. She had to put some distance between them and get herself out of here as soon as possible.

She rinsed her hair and managed to get out, dry off and redress without having to call on Jeremy, who remained outside of the bathroom door the entire time. She'd made it plain to him that she didn't really need his assistance, but when she saw the distance to the dining facilities, she appreciated having him there.

He'd found her some crutches hiding out in a cupboard. It made her more independent.

Rain still pelted down outside, making the day miserable. She looked out the window, depressed at the news that the boats weren't coming up the bay because of the weather and noticed the logs that had been washed out into the bay. The wind picked up again late morning, howling around the buildings and finding small draughts around windows and doors.

Jeremy kept his distance from her, sitting on the couch across the other side of the room. She sat and attempted to read a Readers Digest magazine she'd found, but her interest kept drawing to the sullen man on the opposite couch. He had his nose buried in a book. Every time she looked up, he was reading. He didn't appear to be looking over at her. A pain started in her chest and she sighed inwardly. Perhaps she had imagined it. Imagined he had kissed her, held her or…

She shook her head, and went back to the magazine, not that it held much attraction for her.

~∞~

Jeremy turned the television on, so she flicked aimlessly through the programs. There was nothing to watch, even with 70 odd channels. She looked over at the small bookcase, but none of the books grabbed her interest either.

She picked up her cellphone, still no coverage, probably wouldn't be either. But the phone picked up a wifi signal, although it wasn't strong. She looked at her phone and pulled a face. Maybe the storm was playing up with the local wifi signals, but when she put the cell phone on the arm of the couch, the signal faded. She frowned, wondering what was going on.

"Jeremy?" she called out. He'd been in and out all afternoon, making sure she was okay, but he'd avoided looking at her or touching her. He'd lit the large open fire and came in periodically to stoke it up and add more wood.

"Yes?" Jeremy called from the kitchen. He stood in the doorway, wiping his hands on a tea towel, an apron tied around his waist. Larissa couldn't help but smile.

"You busy baking?"

"Yeah, apple strudel. I hope you like it."

"I like anything I don't have to cook," she replied.

"Is that all you wanted?"

"No. Is there wifi in the lodge?" His hands stopped moving and his face paled.

"No. There's no wifi here," he said, rather quickly. Why did it sound like a lie? Why would he lie to her?

"My phone was picking up a wifi signal, just wondering, that's all."

He smiled at her, but it was tight, not real, and his eyes didn't sparkle.

His mouth frowned slightly and he shrugged. "Must be picking it up from one of the neighbouring properties."

Now she knew he was lying. While the lodge shared the bay with several other properties, they were too far away from the nearest house to pick up their wifi. The nearest neighbour was nearly a kilometre away, she knew that from the maps. She smiled back at him and turned her attention back to the phone.

"Must be a skip bounce or something." She shrugged and focused her attention back to the television. Out of the corner of her eye, she saw him hesitate before turning back into the kitchen. The sound of baking trays moving on the metal counter disturbed her.

She couldn't focus on the television or the movie playing. Why had he lied? Did he have something to hide? A chill ran up her spine, but she brushed off any suspicions she had with the realisation that she'd fallen and twisted her ankle, a pure, freak accident.

But she couldn't prevent that niggle that told her something wasn't quite right.

She checked her phone again, but the wifi signal was gone. Definitely over-reacting.

With her ankle up on a stool, she felt contained and bored. Surely there had to be something more fun to do, but with the weather still raging outside, and the fact she couldn't really walk comfortably, there was little to do except sit. She huffed out a sigh, and pulled her fingers through her hair, scratching her scalp as she did. The action felt nice and soothing. She scratched for longer than normal, only because she didn't have anything better to do. She opened her eyes and looked straight at Jeremy, who leaned against the door jamb, a silly smirk on his face.

"Enjoy that?"

Her cheeks heated up, as she fidgeted with a strand of hair. "Yip felt good." He stood there, his arms folded across his chest. The longer he stood there, the more uncomfortable she felt. "I'm bored," she announced. He pushed off the doorframe and slowly walked towards her.

Slowly? It's like a romance scene. She nearly snorted at the thought.

"What's so funny," he said as he crouched down in front of her. Her face felt like it was on fire, she hadn't realised that she had smirked at him as he came over. He inched forward, his hands cool on her face as he held her gaze and closed in. She breathed out, almost a sigh, which she caught in time. Her heart rolled over in her chest as his lips touched hers. Her eyes closed and she allowed herself to let go, allowed his tongue to seductively taste her lips, dip inside her mouth, and touch her own. It was like an electric shock went through her body. She tensed up, but he held her steady, not letting her go. She was trapped, kissing him. The man that kept rejecting her... that she kept rejecting but damn it, it felt so good. Perhaps she should just let go, just once. What would it hurt to allow him to have his way?

To make her feel... What? Desirable? Sexy? Fuckable?

She pushed against him, and he let her, but his hands remained, framing her face, his forehead resting on her own.

"What do you want?" Her breathless voice didn't sound like her own.

"I honestly don't know. But I know I want you, right now."

"Now?" Her voice squeaked and he chuckled.

"Yeah, now's as good a time as any. I can't promise forever, but I think we've both reached the conclusion that just now is good enough." This time, she smiled and nodded.

"Was exactly what I was thinking." She closed the gap and kissed him. He sat on the couch next to her, and she pushed her hands up underneath his shirt, feeling the muscles flex beneath her fingers. She scraped her fingernails across his back causing his breath to catch and he shuddered. His hands slid down, one hooked around her neck, pulling her closer to him. The other reached up underneath the front of her tee shirt, brushing across her skin in feathery strokes. With so many sensations going on, she didn't know which one to focus on. Their mouths joined, her fingers playing along the muscles of his back, his thumb stroking her breast through the fabric of her bra.

She came up for breath, took a gulp of air, and pulled his shirt over his head. She couldn't help but admire the lines and plains of his stomach and chest. Finely chiselled, he looked like he'd walked out of a scene from an action movie. He lifted her tee shirt over her head, sighing as he looked at her body.

Larissa had never really liked the way her body had grown into adulthood. Her hips were too wide, her stomach was slightly paunchy, even though she was active enough. She crossed her arms across her chest, turning her head away from his hot gaze. Jeremy's fingers pulled gently on her arms, taking hold of her hands and holding them out from her body, allowing him full view of her half naked torso.

"Geez Lari, you're beautiful."

"Hmph," she replied, trying to shake his hands from her own. His gaze caught hers, and held it, his eyes showing his appreciation of her form. "You're a real woman, unlike the stick figures that think they are."

"Is that a nice way of saying I'm fat?" Larissa asked, her face warming as she spoke. His eyes remained focused on her face, his face a picture of calmness.

"Far from it, Lari. I was complementing you on your curves. This is what a real woman should look like. You New Zealand women seem to think that you're all fat, but you aren't."

"Oh," she replied, unsure how to reply to that comment. His eyes left hers and once more swept over her chest. One hand pulled on her hip, pulling her underneath his body to lie down on the couch. She allowed him to manoeuvre her, careful to keep her busted ankle out of the way.

Her fingers stroked through his hair as his lips went down her neck, onto her collarbone, leaving a trail of fire that spread to the pit of her stomach, descending further down. She arched her back and felt his body respond to hers, pressing her down onto the couch squabs. His hands roamed up, and pulled the top of her bra down, allowing her breast to escape.

His mouth closed in on the nipple and electricity flowed through her. She drew in a deep breath, pushing her breasts up into his face, as he fondled, kissed, and grazed his stubble across them. Each sensation drew her closer to the edge of losing herself into something big.

What she didn't know, as right now her brain was only concentrating on the sensations, were a thousand different feelings being processed... his breath chilling the skin he'd licked or kissed, his aftershave and his distinct body odour, his fingers tracing lines on her skin, her eyes seeing only colours flickering on the inside of her eyelids. Her brain was in sensation overload, and for once, she didn't care. It was an amazing feeling and she gave herself over to him, completely.

His lips traced down the centre of her stomach to her belly button, before creeping further down, each time he pushed himself up off her. His tongue became a fiery line of desire, reaching from the tips of her fingertips to the tips of her toes, all crashing into the centre of her body, the point he had just about reached. Never before had she experienced such overwhelming feelings, her mind swimming in the awareness, her body alive and sensitive to each touch of his fingers, tongue, lips or eyelashes as they brushed over her stomach.

He fumbled with the dome of her jeans, and in a haze, she vaguely remembered pulling the jeans to one side, the dome slipping out, and pushing them down her hips, with some assistance from Jeremy. With her jeans discarded on the floor, he lay his face on the apex of her thighs, breathing, his fingers circling around between her thighs.

She desperately wanted him to touch her, reach inside of her and feel the yearning that she was being swamped by. She lifted her hips and pushed them up towards him, but he pushed them back down. She groaned, unable to say exactly what she wanted. He toyed with her, teasing her, his fingers so damned close, then his mouth, his tongue, still tantalisingly there, but not quite. He pushed himself up, removing his own jeans and boxers before laying himself down on top of her.

His rigidness drew another gasp from her as it came to rest between her thighs, insistently pushing at her opening. She opened her legs and her mouth at the same time, allowing him to enter into her, pushing the sensations higher with each inch of his entry. She couldn't take it anymore, and she saw stars explode behind her closed eyes as the overwhelming rush as the orgasm took hold, sending her into happy oblivion. Jeremy grunted as he struggled to keep inside of her while the spasms pushed against him, but a couple of strokes and he threw his head back growling. He panted then looked back down at her, his eyes glazed.

She couldn't believe the sensations in her body, her fingers and toes tingled, her body ached in a pleasant way, her breasts were tender, but the fireworks in her head…

"Wow," she said. Never before had she experienced such an orgasm. In the three years she had been with Gerald, she'd had to fake most of her orgasms, or sit on him and bring them on herself, but this one had taken over before she even knew what had hit her.

Jeremy pushed himself up off her body and looked into her eyes. His grey eyes were clear, the iris' almost a steel colour. She wanted to lose herself into his soul. His forehead rested on hers, and his lips met with her damp forehead.

"Wow, yourself," he said, grinning at her. "That was amazing. I didn't think I was going to keep it together."

"That is definitely a first for me."

"First what?"

"First orgasm without too much foreplay, or stimulation."

"Really? Wow, you have led a sheltered life," he laughed softly.

"No, just not had many good partners."

"Well, it was totally awesome for me," he replied, slowly easing himself up onto his elbows, and pulling out of her. He walked out into the kitchen, leaving her body uncovered and cold, and she wanted his touch back. His scent had been comforting, sensual, and her body was still responding to the orgasm, small tremors in the muscles of her butt and thighs, the tingling of her extremities had eased, but the whole euphoric feeling still surrounded her.

Chapter Sixteen

Harley washed his hands in the basin and looked at his reflection. He looked smug, but he had a reason to be, Larissa was hot, and her body had responded amazingly to his, and his own orgasm had eclipsed anything he'd experienced before. Even Brigette hadn't excited him this much. He smiled at his reflection as he left, wandering back into the lounge area. Larissa was sitting up, she'd pulled the throw from the back of the couch and draped it around her shoulders, her arms holding her knees tucked up to her chest. She looked up at him, and his heart melted. She had such a sadness about her. An aching rawness that he wanted to fix.

"What's wrong?" he asked. He knelt down in front of her, pushing a strand of hair away from her face and hooking it behind her ear.

"I... I don't know. You moved and I felt so cold."

"Oh, honey." He picked her up and sat down on the seat, tucking her up on his lap. He felt her shudder and lifted her chin to look at him.

"That was... so..." Her eyes flooded with tears as her mouth moved, but she couldn't seem to put the words to her thoughts. A tear trickled down her cheek. He traced it with his thumb, rubbing it away.

"Shh, it's okay now Lari, you're safe with me."

"Safe? I've just had the best sex of my life and now..." she clamped her mouth shut, and refused to talk further. But he knew what she was going to say. He nodded, aware of his own feelings. He'd conquered her body, but shattered her feelings.

In a couple of days, they would be going in different directions. He held her close, trying to comfort her. Regret already putting its cold claws into his thoughts. He shouldn't have touched her. But he couldn't resist. Once more, he'd thought with his dick, and not his head. He leaned over her head, kissing her hair. The smell of her shampoo embedded itself in his nostrils, a smell he would remember for as long as he lived.

A moment in time when they'd shared something special, a precious moment. He kissed her head, trying to impart some confidence into her, confidence he didn't feel.

"I have to go back home..." she sobbed. A horrible thought struck him.

"Oh my... do you have a boyfriend? Or a husband?" He looked into her eyes, searching for the truth. Anything to let him appease the cold guilt that gripped his stomach.

"No. I have no one. I just kicked my boyfriend out. He was a no good, lazy, loser."

"You deserve so much better than that."

"Damned straight I do. And instead, I end up having a fling with a perfect stranger, someone that I'll never see again."

"I'm sorry," he muttered.

"Just shut up," she hissed, and he could tell by her tone that she wasn't going to let him start with the whole, 'it was my fault' guilt trip again. She didn't need it.

"I don't know what I was thinking, you're so special, Lari, I wanted to share a moment with you. I didn't think..."

"No, you don't think do you?" She tried to unwrap herself and get off his lap, but he held her tight.

"Let go of me," she hissed, her eyes blazing with anger, her face starting to redden. "You just have to ruin a good thing, don't you!"

He let her go, and she snatched up the throw, wrapping it around her body, and picking up her clothes, she glared at him before limping from the room. He heard the door slam as she left, he presumed for her room.

He shook his head before putting it in his hands. Why did he torture himself? He got up from the couch and picked up his own clothes, putting them on as he found them. He sighed and pulled a hand through his hair, wondering what he did now. If truth be told, he didn't want to actually let her go, he would rather keep her close, continue holding her, but with the rape allegations back in Britain, he couldn't risk telling her about that, especially now. All he needed was another rape allegation, even though, like Brigette, there had been no forced sex. Lari had gone into it completely consensually. He could still smell her body on his clothes.

Damn it! He punched the back of the couch, thankful that it was padded, but his knuckles still hurt. There wasn't much he could do now. Perhaps Simon could take her back to Nelson. He must be due to come back out - but with the weather the way it was, it would probably be tomorrow.

He didn't know if tomorrow would be soon enough. He turned and went into the kitchen, which was slowly filling with warmth and the scent of apple and cinnamon. He checked on the strudel, making sure it wasn't burning, before going out to the store room. He'd hidden the phone in there so that she couldn't find it because he didn't want her to leave... but now she couldn't leave soon enough. But he didn't want her to leave like this.

He was so bloody confused. His body and mind were fighting against each other. He knew all the arguments for not being with her, but he couldn't resist her, there was something about her that he wanted to protect, something that he was drawn to. It certainly wasn't her moods. She could run hot and cold, but he also knew that he did too.

He picked up the phone and dialled Simon's number. It rang through, and he tapped his fingers on the small shelf that he leaned on, waiting for Simon to pick up.

"Hey Jeremy, how's it going?

"Hi Simon, I'm doing okay, how about you?

"Not too bad. Surviving okay out there? Any damage?"

"No, everything is going okay out here. I was just... ringing to see when you were next planning on coming out?"

"It won't be today," Simon laughed as he responded.

"I kind of figured that. Just asking that's all."

"Well, the surf will be too big tonight, but it might have eased by tomorrow morning. Tomorrow okay? You getting lonely out there?" Another chuckle.

"No. Actually, no." He swallowed hard, he had been going to tell Simon about Lari, but decided not to. He didn't want Lari to go tonight. And he knew that Simon would arrange transport if he knew there was an injured person there.

"Tomorrow's good. Can you bring in the usual, milk, bread?"

"Anything else?"

"Not that I can think of. I'll let you know tonight if there is."

"Okay, thanks for that. Stay safe."

"The storm seems to be easing, we'll be okay."

"We'll?"

Jeremy nearly choked. "Me and the lodge, you know!", he laughed, knowing it sounded forced.

"See you tomorrow."

"Bye," Simon said, although he didn't seem convinced. He put the phone back in the cradle and turned around to see Lari standing in the doorway, her face a mask of fury.

"No phone, huh? God, I can't believe you, you've lied to me, and you've..." she shuddered as she backed out the doorway, shaking her head.

"Lari, please, I can explain."

"No. No, No, No!"

~∞~

She backed up until her back hit the bench. "Don't touch me," she said, as he approached her.

"Lari, please..."

"Don't Jeremy, or whatever your name is."

He breathed out, blowing the breath out through his cheeks. His mind was in flight mode. How should he deal with this?

"Lari. Stop," he said. He could see by her wide open eyes that she was scared, that and the fact her face was pale and her hands were held up in front of her.

"You could be a rapist for all I know," her voice cracked. He snorted at that comment. It wasn't really funny, but he could see the irony in the statement.

"You could be right, yes."

That took the wind out of her sails. Her body relaxed a little, not as much as he would like, but her shoulders dropped. He grabbed a hand before she could snatch it back and pulled her towards the lounge. He sat her down on the couch and sat beside her. Her eyes darted around the room, but he let go of her hand so that she felt safer.

"I'm not a rapist. I'm just an incredibly private person. You see..." He shook his head, wondering just what he should say. He extended his hand to her. "Hi, my name is Harley Orion."

Her face changed, she looked at him through narrowed eyes. She hadn't taken his hand, but she slowly reached up and took it.

"Harley Orion? As in the Harley Orion?"

"I don't know of any other Harley Orion, but I'm sure there are others around."

"Harley Orion, the action movie star?"

"Yip, that's me."

She choked as she looked at him. "Sorry, I'm... that really wasn't what I was expecting."

"I'm sorry? What were you expecting?"

"A confession, of sorts, I guess. Wow, Harley Orion. What are you doing out here?"

"I'm..." he hunted around for the right words. "I'm here on a break, for a month. Just to take some time out and recover."

"Recover?"

"Yeah, those stunts are hard on my body."

"You do your own stunts?"

"Yeah," he smiled. She smiled too, shaking her head.

"I can't believe it was Harley Orion that made me twist my ankle."

"That wasn't my fault," he said, as she giggled at him.

"Just joking you. But I'm still angry that you lied to me. Not just about who you are, but also about the phone, and I guess there is wifi here too."

Harley ducked his head, his cheeks flushing red. It was all the answers she needed. "Yeah," he scrubbed a hand through his hair. "There is wifi."

"Why wouldn't you let me use it?"

"I really don't want people to know that I'm here. I'm on holiday, remember."

"Surely I could have called for help and waited on the beach."

"In a storm?" He raised an eyebrow, which was quite a cute look on him.

"Good point."

"Look, it isn't often that I get to go away and enjoy myself, I value my privacy. I just wanted some time alone."

"That makes sense," Larissa agreed, nodding her head.

Wow, Harley Orion.

Harley Orion who has a girlfriend back in Britain.

Her gaze widened in horror. He was still lying to her!

Chapter Seventeen

Harley saw the look of shock on Larissa's face, her eyes opened wide, her face going pale.

"Brigette," she muttered.

Harley closed his eyes. "It's not what you think."

"Not what I think? I honestly don't know what to think anymore. You're in New Zealand, a bit lonely, eh. Here's a kiwi girl, let's screw her." Larissa turned away from him and attempted to lift herself out of the chair.

"I'm not with Brigette anymore."

"Do you think I'm dumb? It's the oldest line in the book!" Her voice raised as her cheeks flushed red, so red he could almost feel the heat radiating off them. It was anger and embarrassment rolled into one, and it wasn't pretty. She hobbled across to the doorway.

"You know, that's not much of a dramatic exit," he said, trying to lighten the mood. The glare she threw at him over her shoulder withered his heart. Looks can kill.

"You're just a stuck up, pompous, shit!" she said quietly, her eyes glistening. "You expect girls to fall at their feet for you. To fawn all over you, come at your beck and call. Well, I'm not one of those girls, crippled or not. I'm a woman who knows what she wants, and I know that I'm not a homewrecker. I enjoyed what we had, but that was...was...before I knew who you were. I don't want anything further to do with you -" she hiccupped as she shuffled away. A hand moved to her face, and he presumed she was rubbing away tears.

"It's the lying that I can't handle. I've been lied to for so long. I don't know why I assumed that you weren't like that. I'm wrong, so very wrong."

Harley sat there, watching and listening to her shuffle her way outside. He knew that nothing he could say would make any difference. Every argument he thought of sounded like a cliché. And he, of all people, knew what it is like to listen to clichés. He sighed as he sunk back into the couch, rubbing his hands over his face.

Lies, lies, lies. They always lead to the same thing. More lies.

He'd lied about his name, his purpose for being there, and even when offered the chance to come clean, he couldn't tell her why he was there, to avoid the police over a rape allegation.

Her first comment had been a little too accurate for his comfort. But he wasn't a rapist.

So why did you run?

Trust his brain to come up with such a simple question. One he couldn't answer simply.

Panic was only part of it, and being away from all the drama that such an accusation could cause. The fact that she'd already accused him of assault was already on record, and people are always quick to judge.

He punched the armrest. If only life were more simple!

He envied Larissa her carefree life. Well, maybe not totally carefree, but at least without the added complication of people judging him as a muscle head. That and the fact that he was an actor, so probably had a superior complex from other people. Gossip columns often speculated about who he was, what he did, when he did it, who he did it with. He loved his privacy, guarded it, but since Bimbo came into his life, it had become one chaotic road trip, careering out of control. Because of her, everyone knew his business.

He hated it.

He envied Lari her privacy, her ability to just come and go as she pleased without any scrutiny. He'd run away because he couldn't handle the circus his life had become. If he hadn't been in such a tight spot, and been able to think clearly, then he would've been able to see what was going on, and handle it so differently. Just like he should've talked to Lari and told her everything up front from the start. He sighed.

"Better go and apologise," he said to the empty room. He breathed out, leaned forward and clasped his hands, resting his forearms on his knees.

At least he could fix something now. He didn't like the feeling he got in his gut, but he had to. He got up, his head feeling light. He drew a breath, deep into his lungs, and blew it out as he left the room. He opened the door to the outside and found Larissa huddled in the courtyard, wet through from the misty drizzle and her shoulders shook, obviously crying.

His heart crashed against his sternum.

How could he do that to her?

He scooped her up and brought her back inside. Pulling the throw off the back of the couch, he sat, bundling her up in the blanket, letting her cry as he gently stroked her back. When she finally stopped hiccupping and wiped the tears from her eyes, she looked up, her gaze fixing on his.

Instead of anger, as he'd anticipated, he saw hurt and pain deep inside her soul. It was the betrayal that shook him the most.

He pulled her tight against him. "I'm so sorry, Lari. I didn't mean to lie to you, and I know you think this is a glib response, but seeing all that pain inside you, I didn't realise just how deep I'd cut you." She rested her head on his chest, no doubt listening to his heartbeat, which pumped wildly.

"It's not just you. It's everything over the last week. The job, my flat, my dickhead ex-friend."

"There was more than a dumped boyfriend?"

She hiccupped and sobbed at the same time. "I kicked my boyfriend out, then quit my job, and was evicted from my flat, all within a 24 hour period."

"Shit." He continued rubbing her back, waiting for her to say more, but she didn't.

"I didn't help with yet more lies. I was being selfish, I lied to justify myself, I wasn't thinking about hurting you."

"No. You weren't thinking about me. Like most people, you were thinking about yourself."

"Fair cop," he said. She looked up, hurt and anger replaced the pain he'd seen earlier. While she stayed nestled in his arms, he could tell by her body tensing that her anger was building.

"I could ask to start over, over and over again, but I don't want to do that. But listen to me, Brigette is my ex-girlfriend, that is the God honest truth. I ended it with her before I came to New Zealand, much to her disgust. She's such a drama queen, and I just can't handle that in my life. I want a woman who calls a spade a spade, not a digging implement used to create holes in the garden."

He felt her shaking, her hand over her mouth.

"Don't cry," he said, trying to sooth her.

"I'm not," she mumbled behind her hand. She removed her hand and laughed out loud. "A digging implement... used to create... holes in the ground... that's funny."

"I'm pleased you think so, she didn't find it so funny when I told her straight to her face."

"I bet. Women don't take things like that quietly."

"Believe me, it was *not* a quiet conversation."

"So what happened?"

He felt his face heat up. He pushed his hands over his forehead and over his head, as he tried to find the right words. He sighed.

"We argued about a lot of things. Life, what we wanted, furniture, where we'd live, where we'd go out to, who we'd go out with..."

"Normal things then." She smiled at him. Her whole face lit up when she smiled.

A soft tenderness.

As her blue eyes softened even more, there was a small quirk on one side of her top lip.

"You're so beautiful," he said, placing one hand on her face. She nuzzled his hand, closing her eyes.

The action was intimate and his heart raced with possibilities, yet he also knew that he needed to keep things simple.

He leaned forward and kissed her on the nose, her forehead, her chin, finally her lips.

"Let me get you settled in for the night," he said standing. He scooped her into his arms and took her to her room.

Chapter Eighteen

He lay Larissa down on the bed, then stood back, his gaze roaming over her fully clothed body. She could feel giggles bubbling up inside of her , even though her nose remained snotty and her eyes were swollen and puffy from crying. She'd cried like a baby, letting out all of the pain that she'd bottled up inside. Now, she had a sense of calmness. The pain was still there, but she'd bled some of it out, and now it didn't hurt quite so much. She reached up towards him but he evaded her hands.

"I think we should talk first," he said. Her heart seized and she felt it rise to the back of her throat.

"We both know that this isn't a long term thing, right?"

She nodded, unable to trust her voice. Her eyes stung with unshed tears.

"I want you to know that I think you are someone special, Lari," he reached out and brushed a strand of hair off her face. "But this is only a fling, and nothing more."

She nodded again, trying to gain her breath. Her lungs squeezed so tight that she had to swallow to get air.

"I'd like that," she said when she was finally able to get her breath. She gave him a smile, but she knew it wasn't quite a full one. He smiled and sat down beside her, his right hand reaching out to cup her face, stroke down her neck. She reached out her hands and mirrored his actions. He closed his eyes and sighed.

"Why does it feel so good, yet so wrong?" he whispered. She instinctively understood what he meant.

"We don't have to do anything. We could just... talk?"

"Move over," he said as he pushed her across the bed. She shuffled over as best she could, and he lay down beside her. He pulled her so that her head lay in the crook of his shoulder.

"So, tell me about yourself. You said you lost your job? What do you do?"

Lari looked up at the ceiling, his scent surrounding her, comforting her. He had her snuggled in close and she could feel the heat of him for the entire length of her body.

"I'm a fully trained legal executive, which means I can do most things that a lawyer can, but I don't have the legal authority to sign things off. I had worked in a lovely office for all of about six months before one of the partners died, and they couldn't afford to keep the business going with only one partner... it just doesn't work. So I had to find another job, and I ended up working for a large legal firm, more or less as a typist. I mostly typed up documents and spent a lot of time analysing and writing reports for the junior partner. I was working from eight in the morning until eight or nine at night. But I ended up doing all of her work, and she took all the credit for it. My title was Personal Assistant, but that was only a title. I did more than personally assist her, I did all her fucking work!"

"So what happened?"

"It was the day after I kicked my boyfriend -"

"Ex-boyfriend."

"Yes, my ex-friend, anyway. I'd stayed late the night before to do a report for her, and when I got there the next morning, there was no thanks, no nothing. And as I had had enough bullshit -"

"You told her where to stick it."

"Yip."

"Wow, a boyfriend and a job. What are you going to do when you get back to Nelson?"

"I don't know. I have to find a new job, that I do know."

"Will you stay in Nelson?"

"I really don't know. I like the place, but... there isn't a lot there for me now."

"No family?"

"Yeah, my parents, but I don't live with them, and they travel around a lot. So I would probably see more of them if I lived away from Nelson."

"That's sad."

"No, we're close, but they are never around when I need them. But enough about me, what about you? What's it like making movies?"

She settled in, watching him as he spoke, the way his lips moved, the dimples he got when he moved his mouth. His eyes lit up and sparkled, and she wished that she had the same enthusiasm for her work.

"What do you think?"

"Hmmm?" She hadn't heard him, she had been concentrating on the lines of his face, trying to memorise it.

"I need a personal assistant. Would you be willing to take on that role?"

She laughed. "Yeah, okay, I'll pack up everything and follow you everywhere." The sparkle left his eye, but the smile stayed on his face.

"I can't. We've just agreed that this is a fling. We can't..." her voice faded as he leaned over, so slowly, and kissed her. Her toes tingled and she curled her hands into claws as she scratched up his back. The blood in her body heated up and sank to the lowest part of her body, her groin, leaving her hyper-sensitive to the slightest touch.

His kiss moved to her neck, and up towards her ear. His breath and touch making her sigh. She stretched out, exposing more of her neck to him. He nuzzled, and kissed his way down, making her nerve endings fire in anticipation. She leaned forward and sank her teeth into the skin along his shoulder. He yelped and pulled back, looking at her with glazed eyes. She smiled, biting her lip. He growled and pulled her tee shirt up over her head, pinning her arms awkwardly above her. She giggled as he leaned forward and bit her breast through the fabric of the bra. It was her turn to yelp, even though it didn't hurt, just the pinching sensation surprised her. She pulled the tee shirt the rest of the way over her head and her arms reached up around him, pulling him down on top of her. She squirmed and pitched her hips up to grind against him.

"You're a hungry wee minx aren't you?" he whispered into her ear.

"Only for you," she replied, trying hard to concentrate on his words, but with his hard on between her thighs, pressing onto the plain of her stomach, she wanted desperately for it. She pushed him up and crawled out from under him. She indicated for him to lay down and she knelt over him, sitting on his groin. It was his turn to push up into her, and she could feel the heat and length of him. She shimmied down, pulling his long shorts and boxers down as she did, watching in fascination as his cock sprung up.

She reached over tentatively, and wrapped her fingers around it, feeling its warmth and girth and gently pulled the skin down. Harley groaned and pushed his hips up further, so that the skin pulled taut over the tip, creating a small bead of pre-cum. She slowly lifted up, letting the skin bag up over the top and then down, then bent down and put it into her mouth. The groan became an all-out moan as she pushed and pulled, letting him set the rhythm into and out of her mouth. Her hands cupped his balls and she held steady as he moved in and out, creating saliva in her mouth.

He stopped and pulled her on top of him, scrambling to remove her pants and panties. She couldn't move fast enough either, but instead of entering her, he traced a line down from her belly button to her clitoris, and inside. The force and pressure built up quickly as he alternated between flicking her clitoris and entering fingers inside of her. He drove her to the edge and then entered her, pushing up hard inside of her. Her head spun with the sensation as the blood drained, and slowly the fireworks built with each push against him. Larissa tipped her head back, her noise at the back of her throat turning into a howl as her insides crashed together into a tingling sensation of passion and enjoyment. With a couple of pumps, Harley joined her, holding onto her hips as he bucked against her, increasing her pleasure. Her body melted into a boneless mass lying on his stomach. Both puffing heavily as they stared at each other, his hand trailing up her back, making her body hypersensitive and the nerve endings frying with each feathery touch.

"Stop, please," she panted.

He laughed as he hugged her tight. "I don't want to let you go," he said.

She didn't want to let him go either.

Chapter Nineteen

Lari lay beside him, still asleep.

Her face looked angelic in the late morning sun that finally peeked through the overnight rainclouds. Her long eyelashes rested against her cheeks, a faint smile on her lips. Her hair, her beautiful blond ombre hair lay out around her head, a tangled mass, but still shiny and silky to the touch. A few strands lay between his fingers and thumb. He softly caressed them, without her being aware.

A slicing pain made him wince, it was emotional, rather than physical, but had the same effect.

How could he do this to her? She was such a lovely person, needy perhaps, but that was understandable given the circumstances. But he didn't need any more complicating factors.

And as for protection? Damn, why hadn't he used some? He'd known better. Nige had drummed it into him from the first time he'd slept with an actress. Too many women want to take advantage of a successful actor, and his money. Not that Lari would do anything like that, but then he didn't know her as well as he should. A pregnant woman in New Zealand would provide fodder for the scandal rags back home - especially with rape allegations still hanging over his head!

He sighed as he eased himself out of bed. Sitting there, staring at her wasn't going to improve his state of mind. Nor would it make it any easier for the two of them to leave. He didn't want to admit it, but there was something about Lari that he wanted. He wanted to be with her, enjoy life with her. But he had to go back and sort out the trouble back home. He could try, he'd have to try really hard, but he would do it. He'd have to.

He stretched as he got out of bed, feeling muscles pulling along his back and shoulders. He wandered over to the window of his room and looked out. Their lovemaking had turned into a long night of caresses, kisses, conversation and more lovemaking. They'd fallen asleep early in the morning, and now, judging from the light and the height of the sun, it was late morning, early afternoon.

Dressing quietly, he slipped out the door and down to the lodge kitchen, putting on the kettle to make coffee. He heard the putt-ing of an outboard motor and could see in his mind Simon's boat bouncing across the top of the waves as it entered the bay. Simon would have supplies, bread, milk, cheese, fresh fruit and vegetables. The chillers were stocked with plenty of meat, but he liked fresh fruit and vegetables.

With two cups of steaming coffee in hand, he took them down to the beach, ready for Simon's arrival. The boat surged up onto the beach, a wave pushing ahead of it. Harley grabbed the painter rope holding onto it while Simon clambered down.

"Morning mate, how are you?"

"Good. Coffee?"

"You read my mind." Simon grinned as he and Harley hauled on the rope, pulling the vessel further up the beach. Simon splashed through the water in his bare feet. "Thought you mind find this interesting," he said, pulling something from the side of the boat. A newspaper. Harley swapped him the coffee cup for the paper and shook it out, looking at the headline of the local newspaper, which referred to an article inside about him and Brigette.

"Good news travels fast, aye."

"Hey, we know you didn't do it. No biggie aye," Simon said, patting Harley on the back and turning him towards the lodge. Harley picked up his cup and headed back along the track, with the newspaper in hand. As Simon put away some of the produce he'd brought up, Harley turned to the page about him. He quickly scanned the article, heaving a sigh as he read about the allegations that Brigette had made about him, and a photo of her with a black eye from a previous fight graced the article. He screwed the paper up and shoved it in the fireplace as he walked past it.

"It will blow over. In the meantime, just relax and enjoy some time to yourself."

"Good morning," came a sleepy voice. Simon turned around, blinking at Harley before his gaze settled on Lari as she limped into the lodge kitchen, still in her pajamas, rubbing her eyes.

"Oh sorry, didn't realise you had company," she said, looking over at Simon. Simon's head swivelled between them before they settled on him for answers.

"She fell and sprained her ankle. I took her in," he said, shrugging his shoulders. "Simon, this is Lari, Larissa. Lari, this is Simon, the owner of Hideaway Lodge."

Lari came forward and shook Simon's hand, smiling at him. She went over to the jug and started making herself a cup of tea.

Simon raised his eyebrows at Harley, who knew instinctively what he meant. He nodded and indicated for him to follow him into the lounge.

"What the hell is going on?" asked Simon in a harsh whisper. His tone wasn't really angry.

"I'm sorry. She was walking on the track and I surprised her. She twisted her ankle badly and I couldn't just leave her up there, so I brought her down."

"When did that happen?"

"Three days ago."

"Three days? Didn't you get her out on the afternoon boat?"

"She fell asleep!"

"Three days you've had her here? And you didn't think to let anyone know?"

"Lari was tired. Then we had the storm, and yesterday it was still too rough."

"Does she know who you are?"

Harley turned around and checked the doorway. He could hear her humming in the kitchen. "She knows who I am, but not why I'm here."

"For goodness sake, Harley. We've risked a lot to take you in. We could be charged with being accessory to harbouring a fugitive."

"I couldn't leave her out on the track now, could I? She wouldn't have made it to the next hut, besides, we didn't know there was going to be a storm the next day."

Simon glared at him.

Well done Harley, you've done it again.

"Is she ready to go back?" Simon asked after huffing a sigh.

"Yes, I guess so."

"I'll take her back with me and get her treatment," Simon replied, once more glaring at Harley. "But she can't tell anyone that you're here."

"I know, let me talk to her. Honestly, Simon, she's lovely. She won't be a problem."

"That sounds like a line from a movie to me," Simon said, trying not to grin.

"I'm never a problem," Lari said, coming into the room. Harley noticed Simon blush, wondering how much she'd overheard. Harley noticed her in the doorway, she hadn't been listening, only just arrived.

"So, how's your ankle?" Simon asked. Lari limped forward, gently balancing a mug of tea in her hand.

"Let me sit down and we can look at the damage if you like. Do you know first aid?"

"Only what I need to know," Simon smiled at her. The smile she gave back to him made Harley's heart thump heavily in his chest. Was Simon flirting with her?

She sat down and placed her mug on the coffee table. Lifting her foot up onto the ottoman, she unwound the bandages on her swollen ankle. Both men moved in for a closer look.

Bruising coloured her ankle various shades of blue and green. The underneath of her foot looked bruised too.

"Ow, that looks painful," Simon commented.

"It feels painful," she replied. Simon carefully cradled her foot in his hand as he picked it up, looking at the sole of her foot, the heel, his fingers carefully manipulating the area around the ankle, the toes, and her inside heel. She winced as his fingers touched a tender spot.

"That looks broken," he replied. "You should have gotten out of here sooner. Didn't you have a personal locator beacon on you?"

"I did, but someone dropped it," she replied, staring at Harley. He grinned sheepishly at her, his face feeling hot under both of their gazes. Simon shook his head at Harley, which made his face feel hotter again.

"I have a boat out there, I can take you home. It won't be a comfortable ride, but better than waiting for the weather to improve."

"Oh…" she looked over at Harley. "That sounds great."

The pain in her eyes returned. He wondered if she could see the same pain in his.

She didn't want to leave any more than he wanted her to. He shook his head, wondering why the fates could be so cruel.

Chapter Twenty

"So, where are you from?" Simon asked her.

"I live in Nelson."

"What brings you out tramping the Abel Tasman in winter?"

"Just wanted to try something new," she replied. "Abel Tasman sounded like a relatively easy track to do."

"It can be, but then it can get cold too."

"Yeah, I know. But then you dress for the conditions."

"Done much tramping before?"

"Nope."

"Oh." Simon twisted around and glanced over at Harley. She didn't see the look that passed between them. He turned back, smiled and got up, grabbing his mug before settling back in one of the chairs.

"It was a nasty storm."

"I know. I haven't experienced anything like that before."

"And it wasn't forecast either," Simon replied.

"No damage around the lodge?"

"I haven't checked all the rooms, but doesn't appear to be," Harley replied.

"Sweet. Once I've had this, I'll go and check out the rest of the rooms, before bringing the supplies in."

"Don't worry, I'll get the supplies," Harley replied.

"Okay. So..." he paused and looked between her and Harley.

"Where are you from?" Larissa asked.

Simon smiled at her. "Family's from Motueka, grew up there."

"How long have you owned this place? It's beautiful by the way."

"Thank you." Simon's smile went from tight to genuine. "I bought it a couple of years ago. It was a successful business then, but marketing it as a boutique wedding hideaway has really helped to build business, especially with overseas clientele."

"It would make a beautiful setting for a wedding. Not that I've seen much of the outside, but when we came up on the Abel Tasman boat, the golden sands just looked like they were from the tropics."

"Except we don't have the humidity," Simon agreed.

Silence filled the room once more, an awkward silence. Larissa could tell that Simon didn't trust her. And he certainly wasn't happy that Harley had her here at the Lodge. She could understand his wariness.

"I'm not going to tell anyone he's here if that's what you're worried about."

Simon just about choked on his coffee. He spluttered his mouthful of liquid into his cup and looked up at her, his brown eyes watering.

"I'm... I'm pleased to hear that."

"I understand that celebrities need their privacy. I'm not going to go and blab about him being here. You don't want every Tom, Dick, and Harriet coming in and disturbing the peace and tranquillity of the place."

"Hmm," Simon said. His eyes were sparkling now, not with anger, but more likely with humour. She relaxed back in her seat, unaware that she'd been tense.

"Right, well I can give you a lift back to Nelson. As I said, the ride won't be easy, but we can get you to the hospital and they can fix that ankle for you."

"Thank you." Once more, pain flared within her chest, almost stealing her breath. She didn't want to go, but she needed to get her ankle looked at.

It would be hard to tear herself away from Harley. Yes, he'd lied to her, but she believed he was genuine. Her only concern was Brigette. Was she still the main woman in his life? The idea of shattering their coupledom made her near-empty stomach churn.

She put down her cup, and rested back, her head leaning against the back of the chair. Even if Brigette and Harley were still together, unless Harley told Brigette, no one would know about him and her. And it would be a dirty little secret she would take to her grave.

How she could live with herself, she didn't know.

"I'll go and check out around the facilities," Simon said, standing up and moving towards the kitchen.

"Okay," Harley said as he got up, taking Lari's cup into the kitchen as well. She couldn't hear the conversation that was going on in there, but she figured it was about her because it was whispered.

She heard the kitchen door open and close, and Harley reappeared.

"He doesn't like me being here, does he?"

"He's just worried. He's like me, likes his privacy, he doesn't want everyone knowing I'm here."

"I understand that," she nodded, looking down at Harley's feet as they shuffled a bit on the carpet.

"I'll just go and get the stores. They're in the boat. Are you okay? Anything you want?"

"Nope, I'm good."

She watched as his tall muscular frame exited through the lounge door.

~∞~

Harley walked down to the boat, a cool breeze blowing in his face. It felt like snow coming off the hills. They were shrouded in cloud, so he couldn't see if they were snow-capped or not, but from the bite in the breeze, it would be guaranteed.

He put his feet into the water, surprised at how warm it was compared to the outside temperature. He picked up two plastic shopping bags filled with food items, putting them high enough up the beach to avoid the storm surge that violently rocked the boat from side to side, even though it was mostly out of the water. He looked back at the boat that would take Lari away from him.

The boat.

He looked around, casting his eye along the beach. He went to the outboard motor and had a look around once more. Could he tamper with the motor and make it impossible for them to leave?

Just for one more night.

The motor cover was loose, and he lifted it off. He'd become familiar with the workings of an outboard during one of his movies, which involved him having to spend a considerable amount of time in a speedboat. The motor was different, but basically, they all worked the same. Just a little bit of salt water in the right place would be enough to kill the engine. Just until Simon stripped it down, which wouldn't be a two-minute job.

He looked at the petrol tank, and back at the motor. He wanted it to splutter and not start. He picked up a screwdriver from the back tool hatch and unscrewed the top of the carburettor. He scooped a handful of water and put it straight down the throat and the water drained down into the bowl. Unsure if it was enough, he scooped another handful and put that in as well. He screwed the top back on and replaced the cover, stowing the screwdriver back in the tool hatch. Grabbing the remaining groceries, and picking up the ones off the beach, he headed back to the lodge.

He pushed the door open with his foot and slammed it with a backward kick.

"I'm back, did you miss me?"

Larissa giggled at him, a sound that made his heart jump. A part of him felt guilty for sabotaging the engine, but he wanted another night.

Just one more night with her.

He moved into the kitchen putting the plastic bags on the bench. He didn't hear Larissa hobble into the kitchen. Turning from the refrigerator to the bench, he saw her leaning against the door, her arms folded across her chest.

"Are you okay with my leaving?" she asked. He swallowed hard.

No, I'm not. I want you to stay, his mind screamed.

"You need that ankle looked at. Best to get you to the hospital as quickly as possible. As Simon said, we should have got you out days ago."

Her eyes started to glisten and her chin shook which told him he'd said the wrong thing. He closed the refrigerator door and went over to her, putting his arms around her. Her arms encircled his waist tightly, clinging to him.

"I won't forget you," he said. She shook her head, burying it in the fabric of his sweatshirt.

"No. It's a tramping trip to remember, that's for sure. And don't worry, I won't tell anyone," she said, avoiding looking at him.

"Lari, please." He hooked a finger under her chin, lifting her face up so he could see her eyes. A tear trickled down her cheek.

"You're an amazing woman, Lari. Beautiful, intelligent, honest, talented." She snorted at his comments. "You are," he replied, not letting her gaze move away from his.

"You'll have a wonderful life, and you'll find yourself a great man who will be honest, loyal, trustworthy, handsome, someone who really wants you for what you have to offer. I know you will."

She shook her head again, a sad smile pulling on her lips.

"I'm in my thirties. Life is passing me by. It's almost too late. I'll have to settle with being happy on my own."

"You deserve someone nice, Lari. You will find him."

"Even if I do, I won't forget you."

Harley knew she wanted to say more, she'd paused, taken a breath, opened her mouth, but closed it again, shook his hand from her face and buried it back into his chest. He rubbed her back, wondering how he could let her go, but let her go he must.

Chapter Twenty One

Late afternoon, Simon came in after inspecting all the rooms and property. There'd been no significant damage, except for broken branches around the Lodge, but none had damaged any of the rooms. Harley helped him move the smaller stuff into the courtyard, but the bigger stuff would require a chainsaw, which was on the property, but Simon didn't have any fuel.

"I'll be up again in a couple of days to have a good clean up."

"Okay," replied Harley. Larissa looked over at him. He stood in the kitchen doorway, while she remained seated, her foot propped up on the ottoman. Her pack sat beside her. His face paled with no sparkle in his eyes. He looked like she felt; flat.

"You ready?" Simon asked her.

"Yip," she said, not looking at him. Simon picked up her pack and Harley came over to her, supporting her under her arm to stand. She hobbled a couple of steps, but he scooped her up in his arms.

"I can walk, you know." She replied.

"I do, but it will take a while to get to the boat."

"Am I not allowed to delay the inevitable?" A small sad smile played around her lips. She looked up into his face, his eyebrows drawn down low over his eyes. He wasn't happy.

"Yes, you can, but that only increases the pain. Quick and painless, like a band-aid," he said, catching her gaze.

"I never did remove band-aids very well," she replied. She watched her pack bob around as it disappeared over a bank and onto the sandy shore.

The golden sand was covered with black debris, bits of bark washed down the river. The water, instead of being sparkling blue, was a muddy brown, and it surged up the beach. The boat sat high above the tide mark. Simon climbed into the boat, putting her pack down in the little cabin, to protect it from getting wet.

Harley kissed her forehead, and she closed her eyes, breathing in through her nose, trying to remember Harley's scent. Warm body, hint of sweat, his deodorant, and the smell of beach and salt water. She kissed him under the chin as he swung her around, and rested her butt on the edge of the transom, and Simon helped her to hobble to the passenger's seat, behind the windscreen.

"You'll get wet, but it's the driest place on the boat," he said. She thanked him as he settled her on the chair, offering her a blanket. She declined and watched as Harley stood in the water, staring at her. His face didn't look happy, but there wasn't much she could do about it. He was the one insisting on her going back.

Simon hopped out of the boat and together, they pushed it into the water until the front floated free from the sand. They spun it around and Simon hopped on. Harley stood, the water lapping at his knees, wetting the denim jeans he wore. He waved and blew her a kiss.

Her heart pounded heavily in her ears as she waved back. She wanted more than anything to spring over the side of the boat, wade ashore and just curl up in his arms, but he was pushing her away. And she needed to get back and face reality. For too long, she'd hidden from problems. She didn't have a job, or a flat anymore. She needed to find a new place to live, or at least work out what she was going to do - something that she had put aside because she didn't want to contemplate it.

Simon clambered aboard, switched on the key and lowered the outboard into the water.

"You okay?" he asked.

"Fine," she replied.

"Uh oh, the 'fine' answer. I won't ask anymore." He winked at her. She smiled at his attempt to cheer her up but didn't feel the happiness reach her splintering heart.

"It'll be okay."

She nodded. He clapped a hand on her shoulder, shrugged and moved to the end of the boat to start the outboard motor. He fiddled with a button on the side before he tugged on the pull start, rocking the boat. The engine coughed and spluttered before it fired. It didn't sound right and she turned to look as Simon frowned at the spluttering motor. He turned the button again, but the engine died. He pulled on the cord again, but the motor wouldn't catch.

"Damn." He looked at the motor, checked the fuel tank and the fuel line. They were all connected. Harley waded out to the boat and held onto the stern.

"Problem?" he asked.

"Yeah," Simon replied. His tone implied confusion. He scrubbed a hand through his black hair, ruffling it. "The boat ran fine coming up here, but now it's not going. It sounds like it's got water in the fuel, yet, there doesn't appear to be any in the tank."

"Could a wave have washed over the motor while you were in at the lodge?"

"It's possible, but I doubt it. Hang on." He directed Harley to stand to the side and he tried the engine again, but it still wouldn't go.

"I'll have to take it off and strip it down. I'm sorry Larissa, we'll be here for a wee bit longer."

Her heart leapt in her chest, and her spirit soared. It might only be an hour or two, but it was something.

"Oh," she tried to frown, but the corners of her mouth didn't want to co-operate. "That's a shame," she replied, staring at Harley. The smile made his face glow. Simon got up and helped her to her feet, and assisted her to the side of the boat. Harley reached up for her, and Simon nestled her into his arms.

"Welcome back," Harley nuzzled her neck.

"That was convenient," she replied.

"What are you trying to imply?" Harley held her gaze. She smiled at the confusion in his eyes and slight flush of his cheeks.

"If I didn't know better, I would have sworn that you had arranged for this *temporary* reprieve."

She watched as the flush filled his face with heat she could feel.

"Pure coincidence." He stammered. "I did pray for an intervention," he said, quietly.

"That's it then. The gods were smiling down upon you."

"Were you not wishing the same thing?" he asked. She looked at the lodge as they neared it. A part of her did want to stay, but her ankle needed to be fixed.

"Why don't you come in with us. Come with me?"

"I-" He cast his gaze down, not looking her in the eye. "I can't." He walked in silence, his statement reverberating around her head. Why couldn't he? What was stopping him from jumping in that boat and coming with her?.

"Why not?"

"I told you. I'm here on holiday. If I go into town with you, every man and his dog will know where I am."

"That's a pathetic argument."

Harley put her down on the chair and stood back. His hands on his hips as he stared at her. "It might be, but it is what it is. I value my privacy. And I can guarantee that you would prefer to get help at the hospital as soon as possible rather than being stopped every two steps for me to sign autographs."

"You think you're that popular and well known?" She deliberately made the words sting. They hit their mark. His face went hard as she watched, and she felt bad.

"If you think that I'm all about being a superstar, you have another think coming. And no, I won't reconsider."

He turned and left her in the lounge as he went into the kitchen. She heard him turn the kettle on and set about making a hot drink.

As soon as the words had left her lips she'd regretted them. She looked at the light in the room, the sun was not far off setting. It would get dark soon. If Simon didn't get that motor sorted out, they would be staying the night.

"I'm sorry, Harley. I didn't mean it like that. I just don't understand. But then you're a movie star, and I'm just your average Joanne Blogs. Sorry." The noise in the kitchen quietened. Before too long he came out with a cup of tea for her.

"Apology accepted," he said, and smiled at her, but it wasn't his full blown high wattage smile. It was a sad smile. Once more she was aware of the differences between them.

~∞~

The light bled from the room. The door rattled and Harley jumped up to open it. Simon struggled inside with the outboard motor.

"Looks like we're staying the night," he said, addressing his comment to Larissa. Her heart leapt in her chest, but a part of her didn't want to look on it with excitement. It meant that tomorrow she had to steel herself again to try and shut down the pain and hurt that would come from leaving Harley behind. Even though they'd known each other for such a short period of time, she'd started to have feelings for him. Or was it just because he was a famous movie star?

She didn't know what to think or feel, but it was clearly obvious by the way that Harley went about making tea for his guests that he was happy enough with the situation.

Chapter Twenty Two

Simon sat the motor down in front of the fire and proceeded to strip down all the parts he could from the outboard, carefully inspecting each part.

"Blowed if I know what the problem is, everything looks fine. I drained the carby and it didn't look like there was anything in there," Simon said, using his hand to push his dark hair off his forehead. He blew out a deep breath, his cheeks puffing out. He looked over at Harley who shrugged.

"I don't know enough about motors to be of assistance," Harley said.

"Don't look at me, I'm only a girl," Larissa said with a giggle. Simon smiled at her, but then frowned, shaking his head as he looked over the motor. Larissa could tell that he was carefully going through a checklist in his head because he would point and then nod. She suspected that Harley had done something, because he had a silly little smirk on his face, but she couldn't say for certain.

She sat back, feeling drowsy in the heat of the lounge. A cold wind had picked up after the sun had set, and now, replete from a meal, Larissa was content just to lie back and enjoy the ambiance of the place.

"Why do you close over the winter?" she asked.

"Not as many people want to come and stay during the colder months, and it gives us a chance to get some maintenance done on the place."

She turned with a cheeky smile to Harley. "Is he a good maintenance man?"

Simon laughed. "Caretaker yes, maintenance? Not so much."

"You didn't ask me to do any maintenance," Harley said, trying not to sound insulted.

"Would you know how to repair a roof?" Simon asked.

"Umm… I could Google it?" They all laughed.

"Now if you asked me to jump a boat over the Lodge, that, with a little help, I could do."

"Well next time I need someone to do a stunt over the Lodge, I'll keep you in mind."

"Just keep him away from the track, or you'll end up with a lodge full of injured people," Larissa suggested.

"It was an accident!" Harley said. "Is this pick on Harley night?"

"I thought every night was 'pick on Harley' night." Larissa fired back at him.

"I'm feeling rather outnumbered!"

"Yeah, pommy boy, you're outnumbered by Kiwi's today," Simon said, grinning broadly. Larissa laughed as both men pulled faces at one another.

"You two are just like children."

"Why do you think I'm a movie star? I don't have to act my age then."

"No responsibilities, no commitment," Simon commented. The room went silent. "Just an observation." Simon looked between Harley and Larissa his eyebrows raised, but there had been an edge to his tone.

"Exactly," Harley said, although not with the same joviality as before. Simon heaved a few sighs as he continued to strip down the engine.

They all sat quietly, the fire providing the only sound as the flames burned into the wood; petrol and oil fumes tainting the air.

"The petrol is giving me a headache," Larissa commented, placing a hand on her forehead. The tense tone and the fumes were starting to clog her brain making her feel fuzzy headed.

"We'll go outside and clear your head shall we?" Harley winked at her.

"That's a new one on me," Simon commented. "We used to have a golden bolt."

"Golden bolt?" Harley's eyebrows dropped down over his brilliant grey eyes.

Larissa knew what Simon was getting on about, and didn't like the insinuation. "I only want fresh air," she snapped.

"I didn't say you didn't."

"No, but you were suggesting that I was taking Harley out so I could fuck him. I'm not a slut." Both men looked at her with shocked looks. Her face flushed and her heart beat wildly in her chest. Simon's gaze narrowed, his eyebrows drawing down, hooding his dark eyes.

"If the shoe fits," Simon mumbled, turning back to work on the engine.

The more time she spent with Simon, the less she liked him.

She sighed. "You don't have to come out, Harley."

Harley looked at Simon and Larissa, confusion creasing his brow further.

"That's all right, I need some air as well." He stood up and waited for her to get to her feet, before putting his shoulder under her arm and allowing her to put her weight on him. Without turning back, they left the room.

"Want a cuppa or a milo?"

"No, thanks." She smiled at him. He helped her out the back door where she led him to a seat on the porch. She sat and waited as Harley lowered himself beside her.

They sat in silence, watching the wind shuffle leaves across the courtyard, circling around the air currents from under the porch. A sliver of moon glistened between the branches of the trees surrounding the Lodge. The breeze was cold, but between the two of them, the silence was comfortable and warm.

Too warm.

She shuddered, wrapping her arms around her waist. An arm reached over her shoulder and tucked her in against his body. She rested her head on his shoulder, aware of the muscles bunching and tensing under her head.

"I don't want to go," she said. She turned to look at Harley, their gazes collided.

"I don't want you to leave," he said, his lips brushing across her forehead. "But your ankle needs looking at. Best you get it checked. Perhaps Simon can bring you back out."

"I don't think Simon would be terribly impressed with that idea," Larissa said, sighing.

"He does seem to have it in for you, doesn't he?"

"What's up with him?"

"I don't know. I guess he doesn't want the place trashed."

Larissa sniggered. "As if I could cause much damage."

Harley chuckled. "I guess you're right. He's just protective, I guess. I am supposed to be here incognito. Having it known that a celebrity is staying at the lodge during the offseason could create more hassles I guess."

"You could give me your mobile phone number?" Harley suggested.

"I could," Larissa said, smiling at him. "Will you ring me?"

"While I'm in New Zealand, yeah."

Her smile faltered, and she felt the tears rush to her eyes. "But when you get back to England?"

He hugged her tighter. "I can't make any promises."

She nodded. "I understand," she said but she didn't. If the chemistry between them was so magical, why couldn't it transcend the continents? Why couldn't he commit to her?

Because he's a movie star, and only after one thing. But then, you are only after it too.

But did she only want a fling? Her heart had somehow got invested in this... what was it? It wasn't a relationship... or was it? She'd come on this tramp to escape her boring life and the problems that were still waiting for her. She'd found herself injured and falling for a man, who lied to her. Her head was spinning from trying to sort out all of the problems that were going on.

Harley was a fling.

Something to forget Boring Gerald.
But did it have to be Harley Orion?

~∞~

Harley could feel her heart beat under his elbow. He wanted to hold her close and not let her go.

But her ankle needed looking at.

Her attitude to life...

She is another complication...

He still hadn't told her the truth. And it hung over him. He should tell her, explain to her precisely why he was hiding away because it wasn't fair for her not to know.

Except she wouldn't appreciate you lying to her. But the longer you leave it, the bigger the consequences will be.

He couldn't tell her. He wanted her to remember him fondly. Not treat him like a leper. Especially since it concerned rape.

She rested her head on his chest, settling herself against him. He felt his body respond to her, in ways that he hadn't experienced before.

And it wasn't his lower body that was responding.

Chapter Twenty Three

Larissa sat on the edge of the bed. Her face hot and flushed with embarrassment.

Once more she had fallen into bed with Harley, and once again she had to face the fact that she would be leaving.

This morning.

She buried her face in her hands, hoping the pain of her breaking heart would go away. How could she have feelings for a man she'd just met?

Harley had gotten up and said he would make breakfast in bed for her, but she couldn't stand it.

She didn't want to be fussed over.

Hobbling, she made it into the shower, turned on the water, testing it on her wrist periodically as she slowly and awkwardly undressed. She stepped underneath the water and let it sluice down her body, warming her. She moved to let the water run over her head, allowing the water to hide the tears that flowed down her cheeks.

Why did she have to have this accident? She could've been home by now if she hadn't fallen and done something her to ankle.

But then she wouldn't have met Harley.

You wish you hadn't met Harley.

She towelled herself off and dressed quickly in her clothes from last night. She hurried to her room, pulling her pack open and getting clean clothes out to wear. Simon had pulled her pack from the boat and dumped it in her room last night before starting on rebuilding the motor. That was the other thing, why was Simon so standoffish with her?

She threw her old clothes into the pack, buckling it back up. She would need Simon or Harley to carry the pack to the boat for her because she couldn't manage the weight of it as she attempted to walk to the Lodge.

Harley was coming out of the kitchen as she limped up to the lodge.

"Oh, here's breakfast." He looked crestfallen.

"Thanks. I'll have it inside." She deliberately kept her voice cold.

"Okay, here, let me help you."

"No, it's alright, I've got it," she said, limping past him and sitting at the breakfast bar. Simon leaned against the bench, sipping on his coffee. She could tell he was watching their interaction with interest, a slight smirk pulled on the corner of his mouth. Harley hesitantly put the plate down in front of her, scrambled eggs with salmon and chives on toast. It smelt delicious, along with a cup of steaming coffee.

Without looking up at him, she mumbled her thanks, picked up her utensils and started dissecting the toast and eating it.

"Hungry this morning?" Simon asked. She grunted once more, avoiding talking to either of them. She just wanted to get out of there, away from the heartache that echoed within her chest. The pain she had never known before.

"We have to wait for the tide," Simon said.

She thought her insides were going to come out. She put down the fork and stared at the food. Her face felt cold and prickly.

"How much longer?" Her voice sounded small, even to herself. She refused to look up, instead concentrating on the eggs. She picked up the cup, wrapping her fingers around it, trying to warm them up.

"High tide is in about an hour's time."

She nodded, trying to keep the contents within her stomach. She sipped at the coffee, burning her mouth on the hot liquid.

An hour.

One whole hour.

She excused herself and limped into the lounge. She heard footsteps following her, a hand touching her shoulder.

"I'm fine," she said before turning around to sit down. Harley's hand fell to his side, his face blank. Whatever he was feeling, she couldn't tell. He was keeping his emotions close to his chest. And she was determined not to show how she felt either. Inside she was hurting, but externally, she wasn't going to let him know how much it was costing her.

"My stomach's a little queasy, that's all," she said, trying to smile at him, but it probably came off as a grimace.

Harley went to say something, but she cut him off. "Can you get my pack for me?"

"Um, yeah." He turned and walked off.

She was pleased he left her to it. Her insides were churning badly. Her heart was splintering, but she held it together. It was only a fling.

Simon sauntered into the room. "What's up?"

"Nothing, just not feeling well."

"Sea sick? You haven't even got on the boat yet."

"You don't like me. I mean, I'm not trying to make friends, but you've been rather snarky with me since you found out I was here."

Simon looked at her, then turned his attention to the open fireplace. He studied the flames before bending down and putting another log on the fire.

"Sorry. Don't mean to be standoffish."

"Well, I'm leaving soon. You have my assurances I won't be telling anyone who's here."

"That would be much appreciated. What is going on between you two anyway?"

"Nothing, now."

"But there was?"

"Not really. Just a fling. That's all. I'll be pleased to get back to humanity. This place is starting to get on my nerves."

She could tell she'd upset him because his back went straight.

"It's a lovely place, but I'm over Harley. I want to return to my normal life."

"You have a normal life? Do you honestly believe you can leave him behind and move on like nothing happened?"

"I don't know," she replied, staring down at her coffee. She knew in her heart that she would never forget the last three days. How could she?

"All I know is I have some things I need to do when I get back to Nelson, like find somewhere to live, find a job. Clear my debts."

"I hope you aren't going to sell your story," his voice was gruff.

"I've promised I won't."

"A woman's promise is nothing." Simon scowled.

"What's your problem? Do you not like women? Jealous that I got Harley and you didn't?"

"Not at all. Just careful. I've had my fair share of *women* trying to get money out of me."

"I won't be one of them," she said.

"Won't be one of what?" Harley asked, dropping her pack onto the chair next to her.

"I won't be spilling the beans to the media about us," she replied, using a cool tone. "Simon is worried that I'm going to use you to make money."

Harley looked at Simon and her, his face pale.

"I've promised you I won't, you'll just have to believe me."

Both men laughed, but it held no humour.

"Is the tide in yet?" she asked, her cheeks hot from their laughter.

"Not quite, but I'll go and check on the boat. I'll take the motor down and put it on. Wanna come with me, Harley?"

Harley shook his head. Simon shrugged as he put down his cup on the mantle above the fire and hefted the outboard motor into his arms. Harley opened the door for him, and he headed off.

Harley turned and looked at her, his gaze probing her face, looking for clues. She straightened her back, trying to push all the emotions down inside, crushing them down so that they wouldn't explode. She could do that when she was on her own.

"Goodbye, Harley."

"It doesn't have to be this way. You could stay with me."

"My ankle is busted, Harley. I need to get it fixed if they still can."

"Of course they can; modern medicine and all."

"I don't have health insurance. I have to go through the public system." Her voice was gruff with pent up emotion. Harley took a step towards her.

"Please don't, Harley. I can't do this. I can't say goodbye again."

"But -"

"No. Just go and leave me be, please."

Pain etched his face. His shoulders slumped and he wrung his hands. "Okay." He looked at her for a moment longer, then left the room.

She relaxed her shoulders, and the tight ball of emotions she kept contained within her started to release.

A tingle in her nose made her eyes sting, and a tear fell down her cheek.

Chapter Twenty Four

The boat bobbed on the tide, the motor idling as it sat in the water. Simon lifted her into the boat and she hobbled over to the seat. Harley passed up her pack and looked at her. Her face was stoic, no smile, no sadness. Her words echoed through his mind.

I can't say goodbye again.

He didn't want to say goodbye either, but he couldn't go with her. He stood in the cold water, his jeans rolled up to his knees, the water lapping at his ankles, numbing his feet. He crossed his arms over his chest, trying to keep the ache inside, and not let it show on his face. How could a woman get under his skin so fast?

"Ready?" he called out to Simon. Simon glanced up at him, then turned and looked over his shoulder.

The noise of another boat drifted to his own ears. He studied the horizon and saw a boat bouncing across the waves towards them. It was moving fairly fast as it came around the point and headed towards them.

"Haven't seen one of them in a while," Simon said.

"What?"

"Police vessel."

Harley felt his face and body freeze, dread rippling down his spine. He hoped he had enough growth on his face to hide his real identity.

"Oh," he turned to head back up the beach when two people emerged from the track up to the lodge. They pointed down to them on the beach and waved out. Harley heard Simon mutter under his breath. The two people came down the track and approached them. As they drew nearer, Harley recognised the danger he was now in. The two trampers were Police officers, one a woman, the other a thickset man. He swallowed hard, trying to keep his coffee in his stomach. He looked over at Simon and Lari, and even her face was pale.

"Hi there," the officer called out. Harley waved to him, but put his hand on the front of the runabout, his head was spinning, he had to hold on to keep his balance.

"We've just come off the track, I'm Sergeant Lochlan O'Farrel, and this is Constable Lucy Stratton." He looked up at Simon and Larissa in the boat. "Are you Larissa Greene?" he asked.

Lari nodded, her mouth opening and closing as if trying to form words.

"Oh thank goodness. We've been evacuating the huts, and found your note in the intentions book, but there was nothing at the Bark Bay Hut. We were worried about you."

The noise of another vessel overtook their voices as the police vessel pulled up alongside Simon's stabicraft.

"Morning Simon," said the uniformed man in the police vessel as he saluted Simon.

"Good morning, Frank."

"Sir, we've found Larissa Greene," said O'Farrel.

"Oh good. Who's your friend?" He nodded over to Harley who remained leaning on the hull of Simon's boat. With each passing second, his heart thumped so hard and fast, it threatened to come out of his mouth.

"My name is Jeremy Ryder," Harley said. Larissa's eyes grew wide, but she nodded imperceptibly.

"Jeremy? Where you from?" asked Constable Stratton.

"The United Kingdom," he said.

"Hey, you look a lot like Harley Orion," she said, studying him through narrowed eyes.

"I get told that a lot," he said. He couldn't smile because he knew that would give him away.

"Are you sure?" the woman asked. "No, I'm sure you're Harley Orion."

"No, wrong man."

"Harley Orion? The movie star?" the officer called Frank asked.

"Yeah."

"The one wanted by Interpol?"

The word made his blood run cold. He glanced over at Larissa, her face was white and her mouth hung open.

"Interpol?" she asked, her voice squeaking slightly.

"Yeah, wanted for questioning about a rape allegation."

"Rape?" The word ended on a high note. She shook her head, tears glistening in her eyes. "You lied to me," she muttered to him.

"What was that?" Frank asked.

"He lied to me. He's Harley Orion," she said, pointing at him. Harley felt his heart shatter with each stab of her finger.

"Lari, please."

"No, Harley. You told me you were here on a break. Rape? Who did you rape? Some poor girl that you tripped up on a track somewhere?"

"His girlfriend," Frank said.

"Girlfriend?"

Harley wanted the water to swallow him up.

"Lari, I can explain," he said.

"No, you can't. You've had plenty of time to explain. No, it's too late for that now."

"Harley Orion, you are under arrest." Sargent O'Farrel said, moving towards him. He looked around for an escape, but couldn't see anywhere he could get away from the police. He walked out of the water towards O'Farrel, holding out his wrists.

"You don't need cuffs just yet."

"Simon, you in on this?"

"No, Frank. He applied for the caretaker's position, I took him on to look after this place for me over the winter. I knew him as Jeremy Ryder."

Harley watched as the grey-haired policeman glared at Simon. He hadn't wanted to get Simon in trouble.

He nodded. "I told him I was Jeremy Ryder, which is my birth name. I applied for the position and he gave it to me."

"Okay, and you?"

"I was walking the track. He surprised me and I twisted my ankle." Frank leaned over the side of the vessel to look at her foot, which was bound up with bandages."

"Did you know he was Harley Orion?"

"Not initially, but he eventually told me who he was." Her voice trembled. She swallowed hard, choking back a sob. "He told me he was here on vacation, and that he had split up with his girlfriend."

Harley couldn't take the look on her face, the pain in her eyes. Her skin was pale, and her eyes were haunted and glistened with tears. Each word she spoke tore his heart to shreds.

He couldn't forgive himself. He should have told her. The truth always pays, yet he'd been too scared that she would walk off, and he hadn't wanted that. He wanted her.

He wanted her.

Those words echoed through his head.

"Right Mr Orion, in you get," Sargent O'Farrel said, taking Harley by the arm and moving him towards the police boat. He climbed in, O'Farrel climbing in behind him. "You have the right to remain silent. You do not have to make any statement. Anything you say will be recorded and may be given in evidence in court. You have the right to speak with a lawyer without delay and in private before deciding to answer any questions. Police have a list of lawyers you may speak to for free." The words sank into his brain like stones sinking in a pond. Each word spreading ripples through his broken heart.

"Miss," Frank said, but Harley noticed she wasn't really taking much notice. Simon nudged her and she looked over at the older policeman.

"You'll need to hop in here too, we'll take you back to Nelson and get you to the hospital."

"I don't want to be anywhere near him. I don't even want to talk with him."

"You don't have to, you can lie down in the cabin if you want."

Frank held out his hand to her. Simon eased her over the side of his boat, careful not to let the boats bang together and pitch her as she shuffled her way into the cabin of the Police vessel. Harley looked after her, willing her to look at him, but she wouldn't. Simon passed her pack over, and Harley took it.

"I'll go and lock up then," Simon said, shaking hands with Frank.

"You'll need to come in and make a statement," Frank said sternly.

"Why?"

"We just want to confirm that you weren't harbouring an international fugitive." Harley watched as Simon raised his eyes.

"I swear sir, that Simon didn't know who I was."

"That's all well and good, but it is your word against his. We need his statement just to clarify that point." Frank nodded to Simon as he hopped off his boat. Together, he and Sargent Stratton pushed the larger vessel out into deeper water.

Harley looked at the beach and the track that led back to the lodge.

The only time in his life he'd felt free.

The first time he had felt love.

And lost it.

Chapter Twenty Five

Larissa sat back in the cabin, Sargent O'Farrel sat against the opposite wall. Neither Frank nor Harley came into the cabin, which suited her.

Her heart lay in cold hard pieces, shattered by the news that Harley Orion was a rapist and still had a girlfriend. Even after he had promised that he was no longer with Brigette.

And the fact he had raped her? She shuddered as she thought about what he had done to her body, the emotions, and the orgasms. It was enough to make her want to throw up. She swallowed down the horrible taste at the back of her throat; and the cold lump that sat in her stomach. She wrapped her arms around her knees, bringing them in tight to her chest. She didn't care that her ankle hurt. It wasn't as painful as the ball of hurt that now resided in her chest where her heart had been.

The door to the cabin slid open and the fresh sea air wafted over her. She didn't lift her head because she knew who it was, but she didn't want to see him or talk to him. The cushion of the seat beside her depressed as he sat down.

"Don't touch me," she growled as she heard fabric shuffling, and knew that he was going to put his arm around her.

"Don't talk to me either," she said as she heard his intake of breath.

"I want to apologise -"

"Too late for that." She cut him off.

"It might be. I should've told you earlier."

127

"Too right you should have. Truth doesn't hurt anywhere near as much as lies do. Was I just a fuck to you. No, don't answer that, I don't want to know."

"I -"

"Leave. Me. Alone!"

Silence filled the space and he fidgeted uncomfortably beside her.

"Mr O'Farrel, could you please remove him from the cabin, or take me outside. I don't want to be near him."

The police officer stood up and moved over to her side.

"Are you sure?"

"Never been surer of anything in my life," she said as she looked up at the officer. His face was kind, his gaze penetrating her own. He looked over at Harley briefly, then back to her, his eyes full of empathy. He held out his hand, which she took hold of, and used to pull herself up out of the seat. He braced her shoulders with his own and helped her to walk to the sliding door then out of the cabin.

"You can sit up with the Commander if you like," he said, pointing to a small ladder leading to a top deck.

"As long as he keeps away from me," she said, nodding towards the cabin, "I'll be fine. Thanks."

The officer helped her over to the ladder, and she managed to get herself up with the minimum of effort. She hobbled across the slightly curved deck to sit in the chair next to the Commander, as he headed the vessel back to Nelson. Salt spray brushed her cold face, making it feel like it was freezing. Even with a sweatshirt on, the cold breeze passed through the layers she wore.

"You alright, Miss?" Frank's voice was quieter than earlier.

"Yes sir," she replied.

She wiped a tear from her cheek.

"Does it hurt?"

"My ankle, yes."

"I wasn't talking about your ankle."

She sat in silence, contemplating what he said. "He didn't rape me."

"That's not what I meant either. Look, I'm a father, I have a daughter and I've seen that look. It's called heartbreak."

She turned her head away and looked out at the horizon, lumps and small white dots highlighted by the backdrop of blue skies.

Was it heartbreak?

Why would it be? She didn't love him. It was just meant to be a 'one night stand' that lasted a couple of nights. There was supposed to be no emotion involved.

So why did it hurt?

"I'm sorry."

"Don't be, it isn't your fault. I should've known better. In fact, I shouldn't have even been on this tramp."

"The good old 'what if's'. You can't live your life by them."

"I know. I've lived long enough to know better," she said with a bitter laugh. "I've spent a lot of time running away from my problems instead of tackling them head on. I guess, now it's time to stop."

"It's never too late. Even for him."

She snorted. She didn't care about him. It hurt to even think about Harley. He'd lied to her, told her that he wasn't seeing his girlfriend anymore. She didn't know what hurt more, the lies, or her broken heart.

"We'll be in Nelson soon. Anyone you want us to contact? Family?"

"No, only my bestie, Julie McNeal."

"She was the one that reported you missing."

"She did?"

"Yes, she was extremely concerned when the boats turned up without you on them. She said you should've finished the track two days after the storm. But the track is pretty much impassable, so you would've been stuck at the Bark Bay hut. You know she's a good friend. She's contacted the Motueka Police every day for an update."

"I know. She's one in a million."

~∞~

Harley sat below decks, his chest exploding with all kinds of sensation, the greatest of which was heartache.

All because of a stupid lie.

I wish I had told her what happened.

But you didn't. And now she won't talk to you.

He shook his head and rested his elbows on his knees, his head in his hands. He blew out a breath.

"You okay?" asked the officer who had re-entered the cabin.

He looked up and over at the young man. "Yeah, I guess."

"Hey, I like your movies."

"Thanks." His voice sounded flat.

If you'd only stayed and sorted this out in England, then you wouldn't be in this mess.

But you wouldn't have met Lari either.

Then where would I be? Another miserable lonely movie star wondering where his life was going.

"Which is your favourite?"

"I don't really have a favourite. They're all the same to me. I just act in them."

"Oh," the officer replied.

"Sorry man, I'm..." He didn't know how to phrase it. "I love that girl." The words surprised even him.

"Yeah, well, tough luck there. Should've been honest with her."

"I know."

"You know, it's never too late."

"I think it's past the point of no return now."

"You never know, stranger things have happened."

"How do you know so much?"

"Did psychology at Uni. The best place to use it? Police force."

Harley laughed. "Yeah, would be too. Tell me, what are my chances of getting into Britain without too much fuss?"

"Harley Orion? Leaving New Zealand without anyone noticing will be a miracle in itself. Not to mention the fact that you are under arrest."

"Yeah, thought so."

He rested his head back in his arms. There was no chance for him and Lari. He'd have to come to accept that. Even if he did manage to prove that he hadn't raped Brigette, there was no way Lari would forgive him. And he had no way of contacting her again.

Best let sleeping dogs lie.

And next time, sort your shit out.

Chapter Twenty Six

The boat arrived at Port Nelson with an ambulance waiting and a large contingency of media. Larissa was helped off the boat by the ambulance crew, who strapped her onto a gurney. Camera's clicked as she was wheeled from the boat into the ambulance. The ambulance faced the boat, and she watched as the media swarmed closer to the police officers. They got off the vessel, and left in an awaiting police vehicle, but there was no sign of Harley. Her heart leapt in her chest, wondering what had happened, and where he'd gone. Another officer got onto the boat, waving away the camera crews, and backed the boat away from the wharf, turning it towards the inner harbour and marina. Perhaps he was still on board. Either way, it didn't matter.

She would never see him again.

That knowledge hurt.

And he lied to you her conscience reminded her. But it did nothing to alleviate the heaviness in her chest. She drew in a deep breath, trying to stop the tears from welling in her eyes. She hastily wiped them away before watching the boat pull away and the ambulance leave the port. Her mind was racing as she was taken to the hospital, but no single thought stopped long enough for her to really dissect it. Not that she wanted to. The talk with the policeman had given her enough food for thought.

Her life was a mess. She needed to fix it. And she would. As soon as this ankle was fixed!

She arrived at the hospital to a banging on the rear door of the ambulance. The disgruntled ambulance officer pushed the door open and was nearly flattened as a blur of brunette hair and bright red jumper rushed at him.

"Oh my god, Larissa! Are you okay?"

Larissa smiled at her friend, but she knew her heart wasn't in it.

"Does it hurt? I was so worried about you."

They hugged, as the ambulance crew disengaged the wheel locks and pushed the gurney out of the ambulance. Julie clutched at her hand as they entered the emergency department, and waited with her, smoothing her hair, and talking non-stop.

Larissa wasn't taking it in. She heard Julie's babble but didn't understand what she was saying.

It had been a while since she'd had any painkillers, and the ache in her ankle was starting to set in again. She adjusted herself on the bed, trying to get into a more comfortable spot. A nurse came over and took their details, taking the sheet from the ambulance crews before turning her attention to Larissa.

"How are you feeling? Are you in pain?"

"Yes, my ankle is starting to hurt."

The nurse lifted the blanket and looked at her ankle, pulling a face and wincing. "Wow. *That* is impressive. What happened?"

It would be the fourth time she'd have to explain how she had twisted her ankle; although this time she left out the part about Harley Orion, instead, calling him Jeremy. At least as Jeremy, it didn't feel quite so painful. She left out the part about the Hideaway Lodge as well.

"No wonder the police couldn't find you," Julie said, her gaze full of sympathy, her eyebrows drawn together in concern.

"Yeah, got stuck in there for a couple of days. The weather wasn't helpful."

The nurse promised a doctor would be in to visit her soon. She drew the curtains around them as Julie sat gingerly on the bed, still holding her hand. It was warm, her own cold in comparison.

"I'm sorry I worried you," Larissa said.

"What's wrong?" Julie asked, her face full of concern.

"Nothing, just in pain from this ankle."

"No, there's something else. Come on, I'm your bestie. What happened between you and Jeremy?"

Her eyes opened wide, her mouth formed an 'O'. "What makes you think something happened between me and Jeremy?"

"That look you just gave me." Julie smiled and winked at her. "I want every last salacious detail. Don't keep anything from me."

"There's nothing to tell."

"Was he cute?"

Larissa didn't want to face this line of questioning or think about him. "He was... um... yeah, okay he was cute. But nothing happened."

"Alone, in a thunder storm, in a holiday home? Yeah right!"

"Truth," she uttered.

"Hey, there was a rumour that Harley Orion was found out in the Abel Tasman hiding out in one of the Lodges. Did you see him in your travels?"

Her heart leapt and dropped from a great height to the pit of her stomach. "Harley Orion? No, didn't see him at all."

"Are you sure? He wasn't on the police vessel with you?"

Larissa shook her head. "No, didn't see him."

"Wouldn't it have been amazing to have seen him?"

"Yeah, would've been." She moved her head on the pillow to hide her blurring vision she knew was coming from the tears.

"Would have been? You're the biggest Harley Orion fan I know, and you say it would've been amazing to see him?" Julie put her hand on Larissa's forehead. "Are you feeling all right?"

"I'm fine," she grumped as she pushed her friend's hand from her forehead. The Doctor decided to show up, preventing Julie from interrogating her further. The nurse came back with some pain medication in a paper cup and a plastic cup of water.

"Hi, I'm Doctor Glover." He smiled at both of the girls. Julie immediately went into charm mode, smiling and presenting her hand for the doctor to shake. "I'm Julie McNeal, personal assistant, Gemini and single."

"Hello, Julie McNeal." He smiled at her, his eyes twinkling. Larissa raised her eyes but knew that it was just what Julie did. "And you must be Larissa Greene?"

"Yes," she said, focusing her attention on the doctor. His bright blue eyes sparkled almost like Harley's did when he was in a mischievous mood. She blinked her eyes and swallowed down the cold lump in her throat.

She wanted to be angry at Harley, but she couldn't. He'd managed to get into her heart, and until she grieved for their 'dalliance', she wouldn't be able to be angry with him.

She focused back on the doctor, realising that both he and Julie were staring at her. She shook her head. "Sorry?"

"I asked what happened for you to hurt your ankle like this."

"I fell."

"Well, I kind of figured that part out."

"I was on a steep part of the track, and I was surprised by -" she couldn't think of something fast enough. "Something surprised me, and my foot went into a crack in the track, while I kept going forward."

Even the doctor winced at her comments.

"Wow, what track?"

"Abel Tasman."

"Fantastic track, done it a couple of times myself."

"I only got a day into it."

"And when did this happen?"

She had to think for a moment. How many days had she and Harley spent together? "Three days ago."

"Did you walk out of the track on this ankle?" The Doctor's eyes lost their gleam as he studied her ankle.

"No. Someone who lives in one of the holiday homes at Awaroa found me and helped me back to their place. Then the storm happened, and a supply boat wasn't able to come out. The police found me and brought me back in the Police Launch."

"Thank goodness for that. If you'd walked out I would have called you an idiot. This ankle doesn't look pretty, in fact, if it isn't broken I'll be very surprised."

"I've kept it up, and put ice on it every day until I was able to get back."

"Pleased to hear you do have some common sense in that pretty head of yours."

His flirtation went over her head. Julie nudged her, but she wasn't interested. She just wanted to get on with the x-rays, the plaster, or whatever else they would have to do, and then get out of there. Preferably somewhere where she didn't have to think, but she didn't think that Julie would let her stay on her own in her flat. She sighed and waited for the doctor to finish examining her foot.

Something to keep her mind occupied on other than Harley Orion.

Chapter Twenty Seven

The flights back to England were tedious and painful. Never mind the fact that he spent most of it in handcuffs with an officer from Her Majesty's Police Force. Fortunately, he let him out of the cuffs when they were on the flights, and he'd been given the privilege of first class flights, but it was the humiliation of having to walk through the airports with handcuffs on, escorted by the Policeman and local law enforcement officers.

The pain in his chest remained with him through all the flights, and he hadn't slept for the two days it took to get back to London. Then, straight into New Scotland Yard for questioning.

He'd let them take a cheek swab after the policeman argued that it could clear him of the rape charge. He'd refused to talk until he got his phone call to Nigel who contacted his lawyer. Both turned up at the station to talk to him. The police would only allow him to talk to his lawyer, Charles Everett, another school friend.

"What's the story, Jeremy?" Charles asked. He always called him by his given name. Rarely had he called him Harley or even name dropped when they were at parties. He was just plain Jeremy Ryder, an old school chum.

"What's in the paper, Charlie?" he responded, leaning on the desk, his head in his hands. He got up and paced around the interview room in the thickening silence.

"What happened in New Zealand?" Charles asked quietly. He stopped and looked at Charles, whose hair was greying slightly behind his ears and a few lines creased around his eyes. Charles leant on the table, his arms crossed over his chest. "Something has you anxious, and it certainly isn't Ms Preston."

Harley stormed around the room. "Nothing happened between me and Brigette. We had an argument after she turned up home drunk and stoned. I stormed out. She rang me on my cell and told me she was ringing the police and telling them I'd raped her. I didn't believe her. When I turned up home a couple of hours later, a police car was there. I ran. Okay. I know I'm innocent, but I just didn't need the drama."

"I kind of figured that part out. Now tell me what happened in New Zealand."

He blew a breath out. "I don't want to. Besides, nothing is going to happen."

Charles stood up and approached him. "I have to ask you this, don't take it out on me, but did you rape someone in New Zealand?" He laid an arm on Harley's shoulder. Harley shrugged it off as he laughed bitterly. "Nothing like that happened."

"But there was another woman?"

"Look, it doesn't matter now. And it has nothing to do with Brigette."

"Just looking out for you, don't want another court case."

Harley turned around, glaring at Charles. "Look here, Charlie. Drop it. What happened over there isn't going to affect anything here. You hear me?"

"Loud and clear, Jeremy. I just want to be prepared."

"You know about as much as me now. Okay, let's get this interview over with."

"Are you sure? We could leave this for another day."

"It's now or never. I want out of here. I don't want to have to come back later."

"Okay, Jeremy."

Harley sat heavily in the seat and sighed. Charles patted his back as he headed to the door and knocked on it.

~∞~

Harley stood inside the door to Nigel's house, his wife, Fleur, pecked him on the cheek, her hand resting lightly on his shoulder.

"Come and sit down honey," she said in her quiet voice. He let her lead him down the hallway into the lounge where she sat next to him on the couch, holding his hand and patting it. Her face was creased with concern. She brushed a strand of hair off her face as she considered him.

"You look tired."

Harley laughed. "Yeah, it's been a long day."

"Want something to drink?" she asked as she got up and went to the bar. He shook his head and watched as she poured herself a whisky on the rocks, and sat back down. The ice tinkled in the tumbler as she took a sip.

"What did the police say?"

He laughed again and sat forward, rubbing his hand through his hair, knowing that it was sticking up on end, but really not caring. Fleur had been with Nigel for as long as he had known him. She was as much a friend as Nigel was. "They've dropped the charges."

Her eyes opened wide with shock and she nearly dropped the glass.

"What? When did they decide that?"

"Before I came back to England." He snorted. "They could've interviewed me in New Zealand. They already knew that the DNA wouldn't match mine because it was already in their system. I'm not. Or rather, I wasn't until now."

"So who did it then?"

"She wasn't raped."

"Pardon?"

"Yeah, I know. She dropped the charges, but because of the seriousness of the charges, they wanted to talk to me anyway. I guess I sounded genuine when I told them what happened because they told me about the DNA of the other guy."

"Did they say who it was?"

"No, but he had been questioned too. But apparently he had a video of them having sex from that night, so they're charging her with nuisance and wasting police time."

"What about you though? They dragged you from New Zealand, in handcuffs, not to mention the press have had a field day with this. What do you get out of this?"

"Nothing."

"But you deserve some justice out of this."

"The police are issuing a statement tomorrow morning to tell the media what happened."

"Aren't you going to sue them?"

"Fleur, you know as well as I do, that we can't really do that."

"What about Brigette? She deserves to pay for what she has put you through."

"I'm over her. I don't want to go any further or waste any more time on her."

Her eyebrows rose over the lip of the glass as she lifted it to her lips. She took a sip and nested the glass in her lap.

"I didn't think I would ever see the day that Harley Orion would be over Brigette Preston."

"I'm over women. Full-stop."

Nigel called out as he came in the door.

"In the lounge with Harley," Fleur called out, getting up and filling up her glass, and another one. She handed it to Nigel as he entered the lounge. He pecked her on the cheek. Harley felt his chest tighten. Their show of affection for each other was what he wanted.

And he'd had that chance.

And blown it.

Nigel sat down opposite Harley and shook his head.

"What a waste of bloody time and taxpayers money that was."

"Harley was just filling me in on the gossip," Fleur said, sitting back down next to Harley.

"So what do you plan on doing now?" Nigel asked.

Harley blew out a sigh and leaned forward.

"I really don't know. That girl in New Zealand -"

Fleur lowered her glass from her lips, her eyes flashing inquisitively. "What girl in New Zealand? Nige, you didn't tell me about that one - come on Harley, spill the beans, honey."

He smiled at her, his mind wandering to the last image he had of Lari, climbing off the boat, not looking back.

Her face - a picture of sadness.

A sadness he had caused.

"I met this girl, Larissa. But when she found out about Brigette's rape allegations, she went nuts, and wouldn't talk to me."

"Went nuts? How exactly?" Fleur's eyes narrowed as she studied him.

"She went quiet, and wouldn't talk to me, and told me to leave her alone. But I can't stop thinking about her."

"And I would bet a million pounds and my womanhood that she is thinking about you."

Harley snorted. "Yeah, like I believe you."

"Honey, the reason women go quiet when they hear something bad about someone they like is because they have feelings for them. Now I'm going out on a limb here, but I'm guessing that you liked her, maybe more than liked...?"

Harley sat quietly, looking at his hands. He did like her, had liked her, *still* liked her.

Damn it.

The pain in his chest was telling him that it was more than like.

"She was something special."

"Then what are you doing here? Go and get her!"

"It ain't that easy, Fleur," Nigel said. "He's got a filming schedule, which is now slightly behind. But I can delay it again if you need the time."

"No. I need - I need to finish this movie, have closure on that, and then I can think about what I want to do."

Nigel peered at him through narrowed eyes. "Are you thinking of quitting the movies?"

"No," Harley shook his head. "No. It will give me time to think about Lari, see if I can get her out of my system."

"If I were you, and this is only from a woman's perspective, I wouldn't wait too long," Fleur said as she got up, kissed her husband on the head and disappeared out into the hallway.

"You know she's right, don't you."

Harley nodded, looking at Nigel through his fingers which braced his face.

"Yeah, I do."

Chapter Twenty Eight

6 Weeks Later

Larissa packed the last box of items she didn't want. A cold heaviness sat in her chest. She swallowed, trying to dislodge it, but it wouldn't move. It had sat there since the boat ride back from the Abel Tasman. Deep down inside, she wished now that she had listened to what Harley had to say, but it was too late.

Hindsight, twenty-twenty vision and all that.

How many times had she looked online for information on him? All she had learnt was that he'd returned to London, the investigation had been dropped and Brigette Preston had been charged with making a false accusation and wasting police time. The knife really twisted in her heart when she'd read that, along with the brief statement that Harley Orion's manager had issued stating that Harley had been in NZ on a brief holiday after breaking up with Brigette and hadn't known of the allegations against him - really cut her.

She couldn't take back what she'd said to him, but she couldn't forget him either. Her heart remained a ruined wreck in her chest, leaving her hollow and feeling like her existence was superficial. Now, six weeks later, her ankle finally out of plaster, she'd made her decision, and it was a tough one. But she was leaving Nelson, leaving behind all that was familiar, and going to start again, in Auckland. Lose herself in the dense population of the metropolis.

There was nothing left in Nelson for her. Her parents had moved to Wellington, and she didn't really want to crawl back home to her parents, they were enjoying their retirement and didn't need her to gate-crash their life. Besides, she still had a point to prove, to herself!

The first week back had been hell on earth. Her ankle was plastered and she was discharged from hospital the next day. It was awkward getting around on crutches, but she had some loose ends to tie up, like the rent, phone bill, power bill, and settling up with other creditors.

Paul from work had called and left several messages for her to phone him back, apparently, he'd found out that she'd been doing the reports, not Trudy, and was impressed. He offered her a sweet deal to return as his personal assistant, but she turned him down. Instead, he gave her a glowing reference and four weeks back pay. That helped to sort out some of the outstanding bills. Selling her furniture and other items had managed to net in enough for her to pay off the rest.

That left her with three weeks to sit around and wonder what she wanted to do with her life. She couldn't wait for Harley to come back. She'd made it plain to him that she didn't want him, but in her heart of hearts, she held onto the belief that maybe, just maybe, he would be the prince in the fairy tale, and not listen to what she'd said, ignore everything she had done, and actually track her down. Unfortunately, the week beforehand, he'd returned to work on the film set. It appeared that he'd moved on, forgotten about her.

With her reference from Paul, Larissa jumped online and started applying for personal assistant jobs in Auckland, a place where far more jobs existed than little old Nelson. She'd been asked to three interviews, which were lined up for the week that she arrived up there.

With a little money left over, she could afford a two-week stay in a cheap motel until she got herself a job, and all three had seemed keen to have her on board, especially after they had personally spoken to Paul.

Julie leaned against the door frame, a glass of wine in her hand, and a frown pulling down her perfectly plucked eyebrows.

"Still running away to the big smoke then?"

Larissa smiled at her friend, although it wasn't a heartfelt smile. "I'm not running away, I'm moving forward. New place, new opportunities."

"New friends," Julie said.

"No one will ever replace you," Larissa cried, getting up from her kneeling position and walking over to her friend, noting the shining eyes. She hugged her close. "No one could ever replace you, Julie."

She heard Julie sob, and her own eyes prickled. She placed her head on her friend's shoulder and together they cried. It felt like an eternity before Julie sniffled and moved away to wipe the tears from her eyes.

"You've made my mascara run," Julie complained, trying to smile through her tears.

"And your nose, you snotbag!" Larissa said, pushing her friend away.

"Why don't you stay here?"

"Too many bad memories."

"Gerald wasn't that bad, was he?"

Larissa smiled. "It's not Gerald. There was work and that disastrous tramp. I just want a fresh start. And we have Facebook and Skype, we'll always be in touch."

"That's not the same."

"I know, but when I get myself a new job, I'll book a ticket to come and see you."

"If you get a job."

"Hey, no raining on my parade! *When* I get a job because I will get one."

Julie smiled. "I know you will, you've had a rough deal here, at least in Auckland you'll have a better chance."

"You never know, I might meet someone famous and be swept off my feet." She knew it was just a dream. No one would sweep her off her feet like Harley had.

"Remember, I'm your maid of honour."

"You're not likely to let me forget, are you."

The smile lit up Julie's face, the first genuine smile that day.

"Come on, let's go out for tea, my treat," Julie said. "And I won't take no for an answer."

Larissa smiled. She would miss Julie and her sense of humour. She was the one person who had taken her in and given her a home when everyone else had turned their backs on her.

"Okay, as long as it is somewhere expensive and I can order the crayfish."

"Deal."

Chapter Twenty Nine

Harley just about missed the flight.

He'd debated with himself for long enough, but Fleur had pushed and told him that he wouldn't get any closure unless he went and found her and talked to her.

It was the last thing on his mind, but his heart still thumped every time her name was mentioned, and Fleur had a knack for throwing Lari's name into the conversation at least once a day.

He smiled as he thought of her cunningness. Fleur studied him every time she said Larissa, and must have seen him flinch. No matter how many times he muttered the name to himself, he couldn't help but react when she said it.

Sitting in first class on the long haul flight from England to Kuala Lumpur he settled in. There would be a 5 hour stop over there, before travelling on to Auckland. It was a long haul, but his excitement wouldn't allow him to sleep.

What would he say to her?

I'm really sorry Lari, I should have told you about the rape allegation, but I didn't want to jeopardise what we had?

He knew that was lying, because as far as they had discussed, it was only a 'right then' relationship. Neither intended to carry it on afterwards.

Would she be interested in a relationship with him? Did she feel the same way?

He had to convince her that he was genuine in his affections for her.

How would he do that?

Fleur and Nigel had both suggested just talking to her, being honest about his feelings, but that went totally against everything he'd ever done in the past. He was surprised that Nigel had agreed with his wife, but then they had been married for twenty years, and still very much in love. How many times had he looked at the pair of them and wished he'd had that kind of relationship?

He knew that Brigette wouldn't have been long term, but they'd still managed to drag their relationship to the five-year mark, even though it was well and truly over by the second anniversary.

Should he tell Lari that - how did you tell someone you loved them? "I love you" just didn't do justice for how he really felt about her. And "I'm sorry" seemed lame as well.

He sighed as he stretched out on the seat and looked out the first class window. They were so high up that the only things visible were the clouds that sat below the jet. Somewhere on the other side of the world was a woman that he wanted to see so desperately. His chest seized with excitement and nervous anticipation at once. He had no idea where to start looking for her. He would start in Nelson, but he wasn't sure. How hard would it be to find one person in New Zealand? The population was only 4.5 million. Compared with England's it was minuscule. But then he didn't know that much about her, other than her name was Larissa Greene. How many of them could there be in Nelson?

A vision of her smile, her face framed by her multi-coloured hair, her eyes sparkling and bright, shaded by her lowered eyelids and framed by dark eyelashes. Her lips slightly parted as she listened to him. A thrill passed through him, and he knew he had to focus on the positive because he didn't want to consider the alternative - that she wouldn't want him around after he'd lied to her. The knife blade of hurt sliced through his happy feelings. How would he cope if she didn't want to see him?

He had to convince her that he was genuine, that the past was behind them, and the future lay before them, a future for them to learn everything there was to know about each other.

Hi Lari. Surprise!

He smiled, but he knew it was too tacky. In fact, anything he tried sounded lame. But he needed to at least get her to listen to him, to understand that he hadn't meant to lie to her. In everything else, he'd been truthful. He wasn't going out with Brigette, that had been the reason for the rape allegation in the first place. And he'd known that telling her about that would not have helped them to communicate, and he'd wanted to get to know her better.

How many times had he gone over the alternative conversations they could have had while at Hideaway Lodge? He'd been in touch with Simon, and he had agreed to let him stay at the lodge while he looked around for Larissa. He could set up a base there, search through social media, contact the police, anything to try and get him closer to her. Simon hadn't been that happy about the entire situation, but when Harley had paid him to book out the entire lodge for a week, he'd taken the money and thanked him for his generosity. He'd confirmed that he hadn't been in touch with Larissa, and perhaps the Motueka Police would be the best people to talk to, as they would know her full name, surely?

It was a starting point because he had no idea where to start. It wasn't like he could wander around Nelson looking for her, hoping to pass her in the street. For one, he would be mobbed as soon as he stepped foot on the main street. And he didn't want the public interfering with his finding her. He wanted the opportunity to find her and talk to her without the press involved, twisting everything he said.

As it was, the British press had printed retractions about the rape allegations, especially those that had branded him a rapist - the police hadn't actually put out an arrest warrant for him. Instead of demanding payment, he'd asked them to donate to his charity of choice, Bowel Cancer UK. Most had made the donations as requested for which he'd been grateful, going on television to thank them for their support.

But he didn't trust them. Never had since the first incident with Brigette, which he had rightfully deserved, he'd been a dick when he hit her the first time, but he hadn't laid a finger on her since.

Larissa was no Brigette. A far cry from her. Brigette was high maintenance and needy, Larissa had seemed totally independent and easy going. Sure, both he and Larissa had run from their problems, but he hoped that returning to her, and trying to set things right would help him to break that old habit. Just to talk to her again, to bask in the glow of her personality.

He hoped and prayed like he'd never done before.

He wanted her to stop and listen to what he had to say.

Because he didn't know what he would do if she didn't.

Chapter Thirty

Larissa sat at the airport wringing her hands. Her suitcase had been checked in. Her handbag and laptop were with her. That was the total sum of all her worldly goods. A suitcase full of clothes, her laptop, wallet, cell phone, and handbag.

She smiled as she considered her options.

Auckland.

She was nervous as hell! How could she not be?

An arm slipped around her shoulders and she leaned her head against Julie's head.

"Okay, chickie?" Julie asked.

"Yip."

"No second thoughts?"

"Yip."

Both girls laughed.

As the minutes ticked down, the butterflies doing loop-de-loop in her stomach turned into swallows dipping and diving.

Her hand flitted to her stomach, trying to stop the swallows from coming out through her mouth. The announcer had told them five minutes ago that the plane would be boarding in five minutes. Part of her was anxious to just get on the plane and go, but another part of her wanted her to stay.

Stay and bury her head in the sand.

But she wasn't going to do that again.

One of the many arguments for going to Auckland was - if she stayed in Nelson, there's the chance that she would fall back into old patterns, and not change her ways. But if she'd learnt anything from her time with Harley, it was that she needed to face her problems head on, and go forward.

Hiding wasn't an option.

And once she'd made arrangements to sort out her financial problems, all of the parties had been friendly and helpful. If she'd known that from the start it wouldn't have been an issue.

The call came over the PA system, both she and Julie froze as they listened. Both looked at each other. Tears prickled her eyes as she stood staring at her best friend.

"This is it, Jules."

"Yeah. Be good kiddo."

"I intend to."

"And don't get into any trouble. At least, not until I get there."

Larissa laughed and threw her arms around her. They hugged each other tightly, and she fought back tears. At least they knew that Julie would be coming up to Auckland in a couple of weeks. If she didn't already have a flat, then Julie would go with her as she hunted for something. They parted, and she picked up her handbag, taking out her boarding pass, which she tapped on her hand.

"So long honey," she said, smiling.

"Take care."

"I will." She nodded to her friend, trying to eke out her time with her. But the last boarding call was coming through. She looked over her shoulder at her friend, scared that she wouldn't see her again.

She knew that she would, but inside was a deep-seated sadness. She passed over her boarding pass to the air hostess and walked out onto the tarmac and into the plane, sitting in her allocated seat near the middle of the plane.

She buckled her seatbelt and pulled a paperback book from her handbag. It had been the same one that had been in her pack when she'd tramped the Abel Tasman, only weeks before. It seemed like a life time ago now. With all the changes she was making, and keeping herself busy, she hadn't had time to think about Harley, but seeing the cover of the book, a handsome man with short dark hair, just the same shade as Harley's brought memories of their lovemaking flooding back.

The book, a happily ever after romance suddenly lost its appeal.

There was no such thing as a 'happily ever after'.

Not in the real world.

So, with a new haircut, short and blonde, her natural colouring, she'd decided to turn her life around. And going to Auckland to get a job that she actually wanted to do was just the beginning.

Two of the companies had interviewed her via skype, and they'd requested her presence when she got to Auckland. In fact, all three of them had contributed to her costs and the first night's accommodation in Auckland... in Central Auckland.

Now they wouldn't do that unless they were going to hire her. The three companies knew about each other, and they were all vying for her attention. For the first time ever, three law firms were fighting over who would employ her. She'd basically been told she could write her own annual salary. But she wanted to get a feel for each of the three businesses before deciding which one to go with.

This time, she wanted to be the one in control, and not just take the first job that she was offered.

Excitement bubbled through her as she looked out the window, and the plane began its descent into Auckland.

The swallows became stunt planes in her stomach, wildly swooping around. Her hands were pressed hard against her cheeks trying to cool her heated face. Her heart raced, pounding loudly in her chest.

Now was not the time for a panic attack!

The plane jolted as it landed on the asphalt and the backward thrust of the engines hauled it to a crawl before it taxied to the terminal.

She took deep, even breaths.

Breathe in for five, hold for five, breathe out for five, hold for five.

Breathe in for five, hold for five, breathe out for five, hold for five.

Slowly her anxiety decreased. This was definitely out of her comfort zone, but she knew that she needed to do this.

And she could do it.

She would do it.

Because she was starting out new...

A new person, with new ideas. Finding her new way in life.

A life that didn't include Harley.

Piercing pain cut through her chest.

No matter what happened, life wasn't a romance novel.

As she undid her seatbelt and picked up her handbag, she slotted the novel into the pocket of the chair in front.

No more trashy romance novels.

Her leg bounced as she remained seated, and waited for the other passengers to disembark. Her own legs shook as she stood and scooted out of the seat and along the aisle of the plane. She took a deep breath as she exited the plane. Humidity filled her lungs, making her cough.

She couldn't help but smile.

Time for a new start.

Chapter Thirty One

The air-conditioning inside the terminal chilled her as soon as she walked through the sliding doors. She shivered involuntarily as she took in the busyness before her. The PA system pinged and foreign accents announced arrival or departures of planes. People pushed past her and bustled around. The departure lounge emptied quickly but refilled just as fast as people scrambled from lining the walls to obtain seats. She couldn't believe the number of people in one building. And where she stood, she had a view down the entire length of the building, the other end obscured by crowds.

She looked at her watch and knew she was early. She didn't have to rush, except to the carousel to get her suitcase. She walked forward, avoiding people who wouldn't avoid her. She dodged and weaved her way through people as they rushed around the building.

Never before had she been made to feel so insignificant and small. In Nelson, she was a no one, but she knew her way around Nelson, and she knew people there.

Here...

She swallowed hard and clutched her handbag closer to her. A couple of bays over she found the baggage carousel and watched as the ticker announced various flights, and luggage starting to arrive on the moving platform. She held back, fascinated as people pushed and barged their way in to get their suitcases or bags. Her own bag comes out through the hole in the wall, and moves around the room, but she knew it would come back around again...

She hoped.

The crowd thinned out and she was able to squeeze into a space and grab her bag as it slowly crawled passed her. She knew she had at least half an hour to kill before her ride arrived, so lugging her bag with her, she headed towards a cafe she had seen. The inside was dark and stunk of stale alcohol. She wrinkled up her nose as she walked past a group of rowdy businessmen, their ties lying across the arms of their chairs, neck buttons undone and sleeves rolled up. They were laughing and talking loudly.

Once more she had to weave through the seats which sat higgledy-piggledy around the room, crammed around small tables. She got to the bar and wiped her arm across her forehead.

"What can I get ya?" The barman said as he winked at her. Her eyebrows rose up as she took a step back.

"Water and a menu thanks." She said. A glass of cold water with ice tinkling in it was produced on the bar.

"New here aren't ya?"

She just smiled as she picked up the menu and tucked it under her arm, and juggling her bags into one hand, took the glass of water to a nearby table. In a new town five minutes and already being hit on.

Or was he?

She felt naive and dumb and very much out of her depth. Her face flushed as the businessmen at the nearby table laughed loudly.

Why had she decided to come to Auckland? Why hadn't she moved to Wellington or Christchurch instead?

Because Auckland really did have the most to offer... a stepping stone for heading overseas if she really wanted to. She was too old for the big OE, but then she wasn't too old to head off if she found the right job opportunity.

She cast her eyes over the menu, her breath seizing in her chest as she glanced at the prices. It was obviously more expensive to live in Auckland! Deciding on a toasted sandwich, she placed her order at the bar and sat back down, waiting for it.

~∞~

Harley stood at the door of first class, waiting impatiently for it to open. While he'd debated his sanity for trying to find Lari, he'd decided that fate would bring them together. He didn't want to consider the alternative. The stewardess smiled at him as she waited for the okay to unlock the door. He paced from one foot to the other, anxious to get to the domestic terminal so he could get through to Nelson. Once there...

He would go to Hideaway Lodge and stay there for the night, and come up with some ideas on what he needed to do.

The door opened and he nodded at the stewardess and marched off down the gangway, following the signs to customs, where he presented his passport.

"Purpose for your visit?" the customs officer asked.

"Holiday."

"You were here recently, weren't you?"

"Yes."

"Like it here?" The customs officer stamped the passport. "Anything to declare?" The officer looked up as he handed the passport back to him.

"Yes, I'm in love with Larissa Greene." He smiled at the bemused customs officer.

"Anything else, like food?" he asked.

"Nope."

"Then enjoy your stay, Mr Orion."

"Thank you," he called over his shoulder as he walked down the corridor into the main departure lounge. He waited at the carousel for his overnight bag. He had decided to travel light. He didn't think he would need to dress up to try and find Lari, so he'd just packed jeans, shorts, shirt, t-shirt. He leaned against a pillar as he waited for his bag.

"Are you Harley Orion?" a young woman asked. He looked at her, his heart light.

"Yip, sure am."

"No! Really? Wow, can I have your autograph?" People were turning to stare, but he didn't mind.

"Sure, gotta pen?"

The brunette scrambled around in her handbag and produced a pen and held her paperback out to him. "Can you sign this please?"

"Who do you want me to sign it to?"

"Susie Turner."

"Okay, Ms Turner. To... Susie... Turner... All... The... Best... Harley... Orion, there," he presented the book back to her along with the pen. She clutched the book to her chest.

"Thank you so much, H... H... Harley." Her using his first name threw him a little bit.

"No worries. There's my bag," he said, moving over to the conveyor belt and picking it up. Several other women and girls were starting to point and look at him. He needed to escape - and fast. He turned around, looking for signs that would tell him where the domestic terminal would be. All of the signs seemed to lead to the exits, so he left. Following a line on the footpath, he decided to walk, picking up the pace as he followed the path.

Twenty minutes later, he arrived at the domestic terminal, slightly sweaty from such a brisk walk. Here, more people recognised him, and were smiling, pointing. He'd just stepped inside the terminal when a shout went up.

"Harley!"

"Harley Orion!" and the next thing, he was surrounded by lots of girls and women, some jumping and bouncing around him. Pens, paper, books, magazines, notepads, and serviettes were thrust at him. He tried to step back and give himself some space, but he stood on the foot of an Asian girl standing behind him.

"Sorry," he said as he bent down to her level to check she was alright.

"That's okay. I got stood on by Harley Orion," she said and skipped off. He grabbed a pen and started scribbling his name on the various pieces of paper being pushed into his face.

After about five minutes, the crowd around him thinned a little.

He glanced up, straight into the eyes of someone he knew. Someone he hadn't expected to see in Auckland.

Chapter Thirty Two

Larissa heard the commotion at the terminal entrance but hadn't taken too much notice until she heard the name being muttered around.

Even the businessmen stood to have a look.

"Harley Orion."

She paused, her toasted sandwich halfway to her mouth. Her eyes sought out the man who was surrounded by a throng of people. But it was undeniably him. Her heart jumped in her chest and pulsed quickly.

She dropped her food onto the plate, and got up, her eyes never leaving the man that stood in the lobby.

Outside of the bar, she couldn't remember how she'd managed to exit without tripping over the chairs. But she was outside, her hands playing with the hem of her shirt.

He still looked good, clean shaven, his hair had even been trimmed. His physique was - damned fine! She blew out her breath, unaware that she had been holding it. She couldn't take her eyes off him, but she refused to go any closer.

His head was down, he was smiling and chatting with some girls as he signed pieces of paper, and in one case, a shoulder blade. He looked up, and straight into her eyes. Her heart leapt in her chest. His smile grew broader as he finished talking to the girls, his gaze never leaving hers.

He picked up his bag and made his way toward her, keeping his eyes locked on hers. She didn't know what to expect. Would she hug him? Kiss him?

He dropped his bag a couple of metres away while rushing toward her before picking her up and swinging her around in his arms. His lips found hers, warm, soft, passionate. An electrical buzz ran through her veins.

Harley set her down, keeping his hands on her shoulders, not letting her go. He looked her all over, holding her away from him as he inspected her ankle.

"You're a sight! And you aren't permanently disabled," he said, smiling at her. It warmed her up inside.

"Yeah, six weeks in a cast, still a little weak, but improving."

"Fabulous! Hey, why are you here in Auckland?"

"I'm - I'm moving to Auckland. There is nothing left for me in Nelson." She cocked her head to the side. "What are you doing in Auckland?"

"I came to find this girl that I met," he exclaimed as he stepped back, still grinning.

Her heart hammered to a halt in her chest, pain erupting from where it had once been.

"Oh," she replied, looking down, and hoping that she was hiding her disappointment.

"While I have you here, I have something I need to say."

"Oh?" Her heart skittered wildly in her chest. She didn't know what to expect. She looked down at her hands, clenched in front of her.

"I'm sorry, so bloody sorry. I treated you bad. I should've told you about the Brigette fiasco, but I didn't want you to freak out and try to run off."

"Freak out? Yeah, well I probably would have, but I'm sorry too. But I couldn't have run if I wanted to." They both chuckled.

"You weren't charged then?"

"Nothing to charge me with. I didn't touch her."

"Oh, okay." She nodded her head. "Apology accepted, and I'm sorry too. The way we left things... I was mean to you."

"Hey, I deserved it."

"That's not who I am - who I was. I've turned over a new leaf, and after a new job. Have three interviews lined up."

"Wow, in popular demand then."

"Not exactly, but three companies thought I sounded good."

"There is a fourth option, you know."

"What?" She couldn't think for one moment what that option could be.

"Remember? I need a personal assistant."

She laughed. "You probably couldn't afford to hire me."

"Try me," he said. She studied him, wondering if it would be crazy to go with his offer, especially since there seemed to be someone else in his life. Could she work for him, knowing that her heart would be fractured?

"No. I will respectfully decline your offer," she said, smiling at him. His eyebrows drew down over his eyes, the small dimple in his forehead deepening.

"What's wrong, Lari? I'm serious about the job offer."

She paused, wondering how to avoid the inevitable. But a small thought reminded her, that she wasn't like that anymore.

"I couldn't work with you, knowing that you had another woman by your side."

This time, Harley looked confused. "What are you talking about?"

Larissa blew out a breath, her face heating up. "I developed feelings for you, Harley, and... I... oh, this is so hard. I can't work with you if you have another girlfriend around."

Harley sighed, looking at her, his face still, his eyes glistening in the interior light. "Lari. Oh god, where do I begin? I'm not with Brigette anymore. I thought you understood that."

"I do. I know that. You just told me that you were here to see a girl you met -"

His laugh was abrupt and her heart thudded hard in her chest, while a cold hard rock sat in her stomach. "Lari, I'm sorry honey."

Her ears began to ring.

"I am here to see a girl I met."

The ringing got louder.

"I'm standing right in front of her."

The ringing just about drowned out his words.

"Hang on. What?" She shook her head and watched as his face began to glow, his eyes sparkling and his lips, his full lips pull up into a tender smile.

"Lari, it's you I'm here for. I came all the way from London to try and find you. I've only just survived the last eight weeks. It was hell on earth not being near you. No matter what I did, I couldn't stop thinking about you. I hoped that I could apologise and convince you to come and live with me in London."

"London?" She felt her face pale.

"Yeah, London. Or here in Auckland, or Nelson, or wherever you would like to live. And I do need a personal assistant. So will you? Will you come with me, be my personal assistant, and my girlfriend?"

Lari looked around her, at the growing crowd, curious as to what the movie star and the star-struck woman were talking about. They all seemed to lean forward, curious to hear her answer.

"Yes."

The crowd erupted around them.

"Yes, Harley, I'll be your girlfriend."

He picked her up, kissing and hugging her at the same time, squeezing her until she squealed and he let her go.

"You won't regret this," Harley said.

"I'd better not!" she replied, her face flushing as he pulled her under his arm. He picked up his bag and headed towards the Air New Zealand desk.

"Hang on," she called out, pulling away from him and back into the bar. She picked up her bag and lugged it back out to Harley who waited for her. He took the bag from her, and slung it over his shoulder with his own, and tucked her back under his arm.

"Tickets to Nelson please," he said, leaning over the counter and smiling his Harley Orion smile.

"Yes sir," the attendant smiled back, tipping her head down and fluttering her eyelashes.

"For two, first flight available."

"Certainly sir, next flight is 3:30pm, boarding 3:10pm."

"Good, book it," he said, passing over his credit card. His gaze turned back to Lari, he seemed to be drinking in her every feature.

"I'm taking you back to Hideaway, this time, to start over. No running away again!"

"No running away!" she agreed.

The End

Behind the Story

Running Away was a quick story, probably the quickest I've planned, ever. You see, Deborah and I were tramping the Abel Tasman. We were standing overlooking Awaroa Lodge at the top of a hill, and she turned to me and said – "Isn't that an amazing view. Bet you could write a story about that."

Little did she know that my head was whirring and ticking, and by the time we arrived at Bark Bay hut, I had a complete story idea, which I jotted down in my notebook (because I ALWAYS have one with me!) I showed her the completed story, and we laughed, because that is what we did a lot of on that tramp. Laughed, and enjoyed our friendship.

The characters came to me easily – I mean Harley Orion / Jeremy Ryder is Tom Hardy! How could it not be? Larissa, she was a little harder to place, but I wanted someone down to earth, not too snobby or snooty, but someone who had a problem and ran from it.

As I wrote this story, the title came to me, Running Away. Both Harley and Larissa were running away from problems rather than face them and sort them out. A lot of us do that. I know that I used to. But now I don't. I confront a problem head on, deal with it and move on. Because if you don't deal with it, problems have a way of multiplying and becoming really nasty.

Funnily enough, it was during the editing process that this became really apparent to me. My husband and I agreed to separate. And it's a permanent separation. To deal with this problem, I made some decisions, and my life hasn't turned into a catastrophe, instead, it has gone from strength to strength. Sometimes cutting your losses is a good way to deal with a problem.

But I am moving forward, and onward, and upwards. And hopefully, this book will inspire you to stop running and start solving your own problems.

Gratitude and Beatitudes

Zenobia Southcombe and **Amanda Staley** – Beta-readers extraordinaire.

Sue Berryman – my proofreader who's eagle eyes picked up all those annoying little things I miss.

Leigh K Hunt – This... this... words can't describe her. Her cover art is just to die for. Thanks honey.

Melissa Pearl – my writing mentor – Thank you so much for beta reading – I appreciated your comments and took them on board.

Tee Ayer – When times have been tough, we have been there for each other, spurring the other on. Thanks for being such an awesome person.

Cassie Hart – My ever busy editor.

To all my fans – thank you for your support and encouragement.
I really appreciate it.

And always -
To my **Son, Mum, and Bobba** – I love that they support me and encourage me in my writing. One day it will pay off.

(Since I wrote this, my Bobba passed away. RIP Bobba - 3 July 2016)

YOU GUYS ROCK.

Weblinks

Many of those who help me out have websites – check out their work

JC Hart – www.jchart.com
Hart and Stenhouse –
www.hartandstenhouse.wordpress.com
Melissa Pearl – www.melissapearl.com
T G Ayer – www.tgayer.com
Leigh K Hunt – www.leighkhunt.com
Z R Southcombe – http://www.zrsouthcombe.com/

Thank you for taking the time to read this book. If you enjoyed it, please consider leaving a review.

Who is Catherine Mede?

Catherine Mede lives in a rural village in the South Island of New Zealand with her son and a cantankerous old cat, Everest. When not writing, Catherine likes to read, draw and work in her garden.

Having developed a love for writing when she was at High School, it wasn't until she was in her thirties she decided to really get down and dirty with the words in her head.

Romance and Speculative Fiction are what Catherine likes to write because she understands the need to get lost in a love that sometimes seems mythical. And adding Fantasy elements just fulfils her needs to create fanciful worlds.

When she was younger, she wrote to escape reality, now she writes it to allow others to enter a world where love has a happily-ever-after ending.

If you enjoyed this book, feel free to leave a review at Goodreads, and wherevever you purchased this ebook from.

Sign up to my newsletter to get the inside knowledge on future new releases

Stalk Catherine Mede on:
Facebook Catherine Mede
Pinterest Catherine Mede
Twitter Catherinemedenz
Instagram CatherineMede
Website www.catherinemede.com
email Catherine@catherinemede.com

CURSED
LOVE

AOTEAROA PARANORMAL ROMANCE

CURSED LOVE

CATHERINE MEDE

A family curse.
A lifetime of grieving.
Jinny Richards' past and future are about to collide. Will she survive?

At 18, Virginia 'Jinny' Richards was a drug addict who fell in love with Dean Bradford. By 20, Dean was dead. Jinny believes the family curse is to blame, and never wants to fall in love again. She has worked hard to hide her past and now has a job as a successful Insurance Assessor.

Ethan Montgomery lost his wife to breast cancer. He's mourned her for three years and now he's ready to move on. He understands Jinny's pain, but he wants the feisty Jinny and nothing, not even a curse, will stand in his way.

When work throws them together, loving Ethan is the farthest thing from Jinny's mind. He's tardy and egotistical, even if he is good looking and makes her weak at the knees.

Things get further complicated when Steven Bradford turns out to be the client, bringing up the heartache and pain Jinny has carefully buried for eighteen years.

Will she find love a second time around? Or will the family curse claim another victim?

SHARDS *of* ICE

Things are heating up on this Ice Planet

Vyvica Karala, of the D'Authian Guards, had to leave her father behind when the Crown City of Althu was invaded by Ch'ar Barakus. She wants to find her father and is determined to retake the city, with or without the support of the D'Authian Guards.

Kelvaras Mason is a vigilante for hire and has been brought in by the D'Authian Guards to find a leak in their intelligence network. Ch'ar Barakus has also engaged his services; to bring in Vyvica Karala because she has information he needs.

While Vyvica wants to save Elador from Ch'ar, Kelvaras is conflicted in his loyalties.

Vyvica and Kelvaras clash from the moment they meet and set the planet ablaze with their conflicts, yet they can't resist each other.

But both hold dark secrets. If it were known, their lives would be at risk.

Will one of them make the ultimate sacrifice in order for the other to survive?

www.ingramcontent.com/pod-product-compliance
Lightning Source LLC
Chambersburg PA
CBHW060329260626
47160CB00007B/2740